We are not who we are when we
fall asleep.

We are who we are when we rise
and walk and survive.

So Echoes the Thunder

Molly Katherine Miller

Art by Crysta Oldenburg

Edited by LauraLee Miller

SO ECHOES THE THUNDER

Cover art by Crysta Oldenburg.
Edited by Molly Katherine Miller
Cover art Copyright © 2014 by Crysta Oldenburg

Published by
Laughing Writer Books
1085 25th Ave SE
Minneapolis, MN 55414

www.laughingwriter.moonfruit.com

Printed in the U.S.A.

ISBN: 0692226060
ISBN-13: 9780692226063

Dedication

So Echoes the Thunder is dedicated to
Miles Neuvirth, who insisted I write this novel and
Emily Dalton, who insisted I tell people about it.

Thank you.

Without you, I am alone.

Contents

Acknowledgements

This book could not have been made without the exceeding generosity of countless friends and my wonderful family. I cannot begin to express my gratitude and love for you all.

Also, I would like to thank my lovely Beta readers, editors, and those involved with the design and creation of this book. This book lives because of you.

One

The lantern ritual is strange this time. Though I have done it many times before, I've never had to do it alone. The metal handle of the lantern is cold, burning my palm with the weight of the small candle contained in glass and its struggling flame. The first time I turn around, checking every corner of our hut to make sure no evil thing found its way inside, the movement comes easily. Habitual, even. However, the second time, the emptiness of the room is unnerving. Always before, even when I woke before Friend, he was still there, not a step away, reminding me that life can sometimes be more than surviving.

I pause, facing his empty mat. It is a foolish thing because it leaves me vulnerable for too long, but I cannot let go of his memory. This is the very first wake-span after losing him and the rise of sharp panic inside tells me it is too much. I abandon the ritual and sit at the foot of his mat where I used to sit tickling his feet until he woke. The door to this room is locked and the Thunderbourne never strike in the same spot twice so I try to convince myself I am safe.

Safe, but cripplingly lonely and hungry. Friend always slept between my own bed and the doorway of our two-roomed shack. I pick at a loose thread in the mattress and breathe in the comfort of Friend's not yet dispersed scent. He is gone, but he is also suffocatingly close. The room has not forgotten his presence. It shoves his memory into my lungs and against my skin.

I have spent too many moments at his bedside. I must get up, go out, get food. I look around one last time. There is nothing in the room except our two mats and the scraps of bedding that shabbily adorn them. Friend's blanket is still warm, although mostly with my own body heat. I let it fall off my shoulders and fight the urge to lie back down on his mat. Knowing that he died there stops my actions more than my own will.

I do not want to linger anymore in this tomb, locked away in the very spot where Friend drew his last breath. I lament his beauty, his kindness, and his warmth, all stolen in this very room in one flashing moment. I want nothing more than to leave this old room and never see it again.

I am already wearing my black thermo leggings and tank top, under which I quickly add my bra. I pull on my gray wrap-pants, which will keep the dust and grime away from my leggings. I grab my grandfather's military boots, stuff two socks neatly in the toes so they fit a little better, and lace them around my ankles over my pants. Looking down at my toes, I try to imagine my grandfather in the war. For a moment, the boots are encrusted with enemy soil instead of sewage dust.

My mother used to say I had my grandfather's smile. Since smiles were abandoned long ago, I now only have his boots and his hunting knife. His knife isn't much to look at, but it is my prized possession; I am careful to always have it on me as he once always had it at his side, hidden. Now, more than ever, its familiar weight on my left hip brings me comfort. I throw on an insulated jacket and grab my small brown backpack.

I hesitate before heading out. I know my bag is fully equipped, and heavy for an on-foot journey, but there is one more thing I need. In our food box, in a secret compartment at the bottom, is a camera. It was my father's. He was a photographer, before everything, and the camera is the reason he is dead.

On the day the house shook, quivering and gasping like it was drowning in air, my father went outside to take pictures of the oncoming storm. He died as he always lived- finding the beauty in everything, even in the dangerous. My older sister was with him. The camera miraculously survived, filled with the final images of my father and sister's lives.

I have kept the camera ever since and do not mean to leave it behind now. It was the only thing I was able to grab from our home before we fled. I have nothing from my mother and nothing from my sister- only my father's camera and the supplies my grandfather brought.

I owe my survival to my grandfather, a military man with enough common sense to grab his emergency supplies before we fled. It was his pack with twenty odd candles, matches, a sewing kit, two flashlights, batteries, a pair of night vision goggles, a radio, first aid kit, some rope, food, and water that sustained us.

Most of the supplies are long gone now. The food and water ran out first. The radio lost signal underground, but had one of my father's tapes in it so I used half of the batteries listening to it until it became nothing but long, stretched-out garbles of sound. The rest of the batteries went to the flashlights, gone too quickly because we were too afraid of the darkness to conserve them properly.

I've tried to use the candles more wisely, and I have only used six. The first aid kit is missing everything except a few bandages. Almost everyone's medical supplies went to our make-shift hospital early on. My mother and grandfather argued for days about it but, in the end, my mother was a doctor and needed the supplies. The rope is virtually untouched. All that's left of the sewing kit are the dull scissors.

As for the goggles, well I'm just lucky Friend wasn't wearing them when the awful flash of light consumed him. It took considerable convincing to let him wear them at all. When he first used them to scavenge I was sure he was going to take them and take off, robbing me of my only hope for survival and my only friend. But he came back, entering the dark room assuredly just to stop short at the sight of me.

"You're an idiot, Little Owl." He whispers comfortingly when he sees the tear-stains on my cheeks. He returns the goggles to me. I connect them to the generator my grandfather built and we feast on canned tomatoes and beans.

I put on the goggles and the world takes on a green tint. There's a part of me that wonders if the world will ever regain color. Everything is black and gray and green. I close my eyes and imagine the color red. It takes a couple moments to visualize, and only with the prompt of remembering the red Chucks my sister wore every day her first semester of high school. I was so jealous that she got to escape the horrors of middle school without me. She was the luckiest, most beautiful person in the world to me when she walked out of the house for the first time in those shoes.

I linger in the memory only briefly and then let the world return to grayscale. Once I have everything, I leave my home- our home- and begin my days as a wanderer. I do not look back. Not once. Later, I will regret that choice.

Our make-shift city is little more than frightened rabbit holes and glorified sewer lines connected one to the other by the old subway system. It had all the essentials of a town: a hospital, grocery store, and church, though all were located in lean-tos and tents so we looked more like hobos and refugees than anything. It was better than nothing, though it lasted just long enough for the supplies of our town to start running out, before the first attack.

The Thunderbourne attacked the hospital first, killing everyone with medical expertise and scattering our supplies, strategically leaving us defenseless against disease, which killed the majority of our population within the twenty or so sleep-spans. My mother was working at the hospital when the Thunderbourne attacked. I never saw her again. My grandfather fell sick not long after. It took at least five sleep-spans for the despair and disease to finish him off.

The Thunderbourne now leisurely pick us off. I suppose there are not enough of us left to warrant a real attack. Instead, every so often, a flash of lightning goes off and one more blanket grows cold.

I don't know how long it has been since the first attack. Time was one of the first concepts to be abandoned, easily so, since there is no sun to tell us the passage of days and only a fool would use batteries to keep a clock running. Mostly we run on our own circadian rhythms and the signs our bodies give us that time ticks on. When we are hungry, we scavenge. Thirst brings us to the deep outskirts where the soil is kind enough to supply drips of water. Beyond that, trips outside the house are generally avoided.

The streets are dead as I pass through. If anyone in this make-shift city still lives, their fear of the darkness and the Thunderbourne keep them inside. In the darkness, anything or nothing could be near. Even before the first attack, people feared the dark. Children were locked inside, kept trapped so they would not wander and be lost. Men and women went mad. Misbehavior was punished with the threat of being left alone in the dark.

My mother hated the dark and insisted we kept a light on at all times. It was another topic which could easily ignite an argument with my grandfather, who conserved our resources by turning off the light while my mother was at the hospital.

The first time my mother came home to darkness she screamed at my grandfather. It must have been about me and preserving my eyesight because, after that, he insisted I always wore his night-vision goggles when the lights were off. When my mother came back, he would take the goggles and take a walk, away from the frivolous use of precious light.

After my mom died, my grandfather would neither let me use any light nor put on the goggles. For a long time we lived in blindness. He told me that if I was to live, I had to know how to live in darkness because, one day, the light would run out. "Light is a blessing," he would say, "and blessings never last." However, every so often, I could hear my grandfather's short, quick, breathy sobs, so I thought the darkness had another purpose; our blindness was his hiding place.

Sometime after his crying ceased, so did his appetite, his voice, his health, his life. The silent days were the worst. There was nothing to feed my senses. I played a kind of peek-a-boo with myself, shutting my eyes and opening them, trying to find a difference between chosen and found blindness. Grandfather placed me near the food box, so he did not have to feed me- I could feed myself. I dared not leave that spot.

One silent day I reached into the food box and grabbed a hidden flashlight. The batteries flickered, but steadied after a few taps against the palm of my hand. Looking around, I saw my first dead body.

My grandfather's wide-eyed corpse, with skin pale enough that the beam of light gleamed off him, was, oddly enough, the last dead body I have seen as well as the first. Despite the many deaths that have happened here, I never saw any of them. My mom would not hear of letting me near the hospital, and the Thunderbourne never leave evidence of their attacks. All they leave is the unsettling stillness that makes one wonder if our loved ones just up and left, died, or ever even existed in the first place.

Beside me, a pop-up tent stands abandoned. A wicked smell overwhelms me, lingering far enough in my nose that it almost tickles my throat. I will never be used to that horrid mix of rotting food, bodily waste, and, in cases like these, decay of flesh. Passing dwellings like these make me wonder if this stagnant, lingering existence is any better than the violent and quickly ending life on the surface. All we do down here is slowly fade away.

I quicken my pace until I leave the thick of the almost-town. At the edge of a long-abandoned subway platform, I sit down and dig in my pack for some food. I am still working on a container of peanut butter- a remarkable find from one of Friend's scavenges last week. I miss him. I feel the weight of that sentiment on every fiber of my being. I have to move or die. Lingering is death. My throat closes suddenly. I can't swallow, so I spit out my precious food and wait for the memory of Friend to pass. I am panicking, suffocating in this claustrophobic world.

My world is filled with grief. I let the tears consume me. Usually I cry silently, but not today. Today I am not just crying, I am weeping with every fiber of my being because I am utterly alone.

Someone hears me from the immeasurable darkness. I do not know why he is there, but he finds me and kneels beside me, resting a hand on my shoulder. The goggles are off, providing easier access to wipe away at my blurry eyes, so I have no idea he is there. When he touches me, it scares me into a fit of hiccups. I try to ask who he is, but between the spasms in my lungs and the tears, all I get out is "who... who... who..."

"Who are _you?_" He laughs, "An owl?"

I have no response for him, other than a shaky breath, so he slides next to me and holds me as I cry the rest of my tears.

"It's alright, Little Owl. I'm a friend."

I wait on the platform for Friend to appear. It is not rational or logical or even possible, but I wait for him anyway. It is what my instinct says is supposed to happen. I wait for what could be minutes or hours or days, I have no way of knowing. The knot in my stomach keeps me from feeling hunger and the grief makes everything seem wearisome, but sleep is beyond me.

Of course, he will not come. He will not ever come. Waiting is useless. If someone could come, anyone really, maybe they'd comfort me or distract me or be so afraid themselves that I would put on my brave face for them. Only, I don't want just anyone. I want Friend. Of course, he will not come.

He does not come. Eventually, when my legs are so asleep that they send sharp jolts up to my hips, I get up. I stand for a while, not knowing where to go or what to do to escape everything. Then I pick the direction leading away from the almost-town, jump down onto the subway tracks, and begin again.

Two

Two sleep-spans have passed and the tracks are endless. It is a mindless tedium that I have brought upon myself. Nothing changes. Sometimes I pass other, empty platforms with nothing more to offer me than more tracks. Oh great, more darkness. Another wall. An occasional broken umbrella or some other discarded, seemingly ancient, artifact. Always more tracks.

Sometimes I sing. Songs, like smiles and umbrellas, seem like discarded artifacts lately. My father used to sing. Every Sunday morning he'd get up early for photo shoots, then come back and wake us all up by singing as loudly as he could. Friend, too, sang- usually when he thought I was asleep. As I walk, I sing the fragments I remember from both men.

Suddenly, interrupting an already fragmented melody, a voice in the dark catches me off guard. It alarms me that I've let myself be startled, but I recover quickly with a façade of nonchalance.

"Keep the songbirds underground,
    where sun nor sky can e'er find them.

Flying blindly, flying, falling
if they sing here they'll sing forever."

I turn around catching sight of the singing
stranger. She's an old woman, older than I've ever
seen down here, with long gray dreadlocks pulled
back behind her head, rolling down her back like a
silver avalanche. Her back is bent, but her pace
brisk, and her voice does not rattle as much as I
remember old people's voices should. She sounds
and appears healthy, closer to life than most, and
that is a relief to me, although I do not know why. I
slow my pace to let her pass. She does not pass.
Instead, the old woman matches my pace without
glancing at me.

"Keep the songbirds underground,
gray stone cages all around them
buried dark and buried deeply
if they sing here they'll sing forever.

Keep the songbirds underground,
still and sewed in wooden boxes
silent as stone as no one listens
if they fall here they'll fall forever."

She stops singing and winks at me. An odd
gesture of familiarity. In any normal situation, I
would ask who she was, what her name was, for a
name is a very telling thing. But it is said that once
something has a name, you cannot part with it.
Since every day in this god-forsaken underground

requires you to part with something or someone dear to you, it is better to forget the names and move on.

"So, songbird," she addresses me at length, "what brings you out of your town?"

Everything about this woman catches me off guard. Her pale eyes and clear voice, even the way she dresses- skirt, blouse, and crocheted shawl- caught threads like spider webs on something ancient that has waited too long in a forgotten corner.

"I'd rather sing forever than fall forever?"

She grins. How does someone who has jumped from ancient days to here, who lingers in spider webs and shadows, who is falling apart at her very seams and whose hair is coated with the dust of skeletons and half-remembered anecdotes, how does she have such perfect teeth?

"Do you plan on singing forever?"

I think about the implications of her question. Also, how long has it been since I have actually seen a songbird? Do I even remember what one would look like?

"I will go as far as I can. There is nothing here, not anymore. I have to find something. There has to be more than this…" I'm surprised by the threatening tears behind my goggles. "I'm tired of this. I want to live."

The woman nods, contented with my answer. She quickens her pace ever so slightly and suddenly I notice a detail I hadn't noticed before…

"Follow me then." She says.

She carries no supplies with her of any kind.

"Where are we going?" I ask, unsure whether to be wary or hopeful about the fact that she walks empty-handed. Either she has enough stored up and protected to no longer necessitate lugging food around, or she has nothing and I am walking into a trap.

"I have been leading a group of folks, like yourself, for a little over seven sleep-spans now." The old woman's voice darkens, though that smug spark still lingers. "There are many people who say this life underground is worse than anything the surface could throw at us, what with the dark and supplies dwindling and the Thunderbourne attacks growing more frequent every day. Yes, there are many who want to go back above, but few who have the wherewithal to do so. Most have families to think of, and it's not like this trek is a walk in the park… for most, this journey is suicide. However, for those with nothing left to lose, it is all the hope this world has to offer anymore."

She waits for me to respond. I don't, for in all honesty, what could I say? The woman is mad. No one goes up to the surface. Certainly no one goes up to the surface and survives. What about the wind storms? The lightning that struck so close together that the world seemed to be lit by a green sun? What about the hail? What kind of hope could there be in the chance of finding one's way back into the storm? And yet... what else is there?

We both fall very quiet as I try to feel my way around everything she's told me and everything hidden beneath her words. I make a list of all the things that would actually need to be in place for a successful venture to the surface– if it were even possible for such a venture to be successful.

Supplies would be the biggest issue. Finding enough food, water, and light for a group of people would be difficult- and is one reason most people abandon each other down here. This group has been journeying seven sleep-spans, if I believe her story, which would mean they must have access to supplies, food at the very least. Water could be found in tunnels not far from main subway platforms. Light is optional. It is always optional. Favorable, but optional.

I decide to trust the woman. At least for now. I finger my grandfather's knife, slightly wishing it was my grandfather's gun. Reason tells me a knife is more useful. A gun would run out of bullets, a gun would be easier to use, a gun would make noise, a gun would not be better. At least I'm armed. If all goes badly, at least I'm armed.

The old woman leads me to her refugees. The sight of them eases my mind a little. There is still a chance her story is true. It's either that or an ambush; it's all or nothing now. The small group huddles over a light source, like a quintessential scenario of hobos.

The small lantern mostly casts shadows over them, but is enough light that I take off my goggles. I make out a middle-aged man with an enviable trench coat near a cart full of supplies, a woman in her late twenties clutching something for dear life near her heart, and another woman with zebra-print earmuffs over French-braided, dark red hair. Beside her is a child with a fuzzy hat complete with animal ears, scratching at his nose with a hand cozily inside an equally fuzzy mitten. Then there is the child's mother, with one weary arm around his shoulder and the other brushing away sweat or fever from her brow, and a young man with only one arm. The last two are strong looking men, carrying huge guns in arms covered in flannel shirts and leather coats. One wears sunglasses. Huh.

The old woman, nodding an unseen greeting as we pass the gunman, leads me to the group. I receive some strange looks. I suppose of all of us, I look the least like what a human should be. I am alien, clothed in military and makeshift clothes, not the salvaged Surface wear the others don so comfortably. I wonder if they are jealous of my goggles.

Our greetings are silent and brief, nodding or passing smiles. It is evident there are bonds formed and exclusive in the group, but it does not concern me. We are here to survive and, chances are, most of us will not. What is the point in becoming close to the dead? It could be they try and kill me for my supplies after all. Although rare, raids do happen, and if they desire my goggles, it could be enough to spark something dangerous. It still could be a trap.

I'm unsure how to measure this group of people. They could be refugees, as the old woman claims, seeking new lives, or they could be thieves. I'm thrown off-guard by the little treasures they each carry. Are they bits and pieces of lives they once lived? Or stolen from wide-eyed corpses along the way? It occurs to me that if there were only one of us, instead of seven, she would be outfitted to survive anything.

The old woman does not seem concerned about the cold response to my arrival, so I try to remain impassive. *Don't try anything*, I try to will my face to say, *I have my grandfather's knife on me. I'm alien. I'm a soldier and I will fight you to the death for what I carry. You better hope, for your sakes, the old woman told me the truth.*

"Well?" The old woman says cheerfully to her band of misfits, which now includes me, "Shall we press on?"

As we move out, no one talks. This is fine by me. I replace my goggles, aware of how this must make me seem bug-eyed and strange. This is also fine by me. I am used to silence, and I am used to being separate. Everything we do is done out of necessity, not pleasure. We walk when we have to, eat and rest when our group slows, and speak only to direct each other or to make sure no one has fallen behind.

The road we take is a long forgotten subway line. In the days before the storm, the subway was the heart of our city, and the most common way to go to and from other cities, since roads were all but abandoned for every non-corporate venture after the last spike in gas prices.

The subway was expanded drastically after the gas strikes and it soon became the primary source of travel. So the tunnels are many and go almost anywhere. When humanity fled underground, away from the screaming sky, we fled far enough down the tunnels that the entrances could not collapse upon us or let in any dangers. After seeing city after city pushed over by the wind, we all had falling buildings and crushing rubble on our mind. It is rumored that every station collapsed, trapping the whole of humanity inside the tunnels, in the bowels of the earth. As we travel, it becomes apparent that the old woman knows her way around. She claims at least one doorway still exists to the surface and that she has led groups successfully to this doorway before.

No one knows what is above, but all of us are hopeful that it could be more than this underground tomb. This is what unifies me and my companions; we no longer see this place as a refuge. If the world is crumbling, maybe running to the basement wasn't a good idea. Especially with the Thunderbourne toying with us. The tunnels are a cage, meant to hold us until we die. None of us are willing to sit and wait for our fate. So we are all desperate to escape.

The subway tracks are difficult to maneuver. The child's mother carries him on her back as she stumbles forward. On my right I can hear the red-haired woman humming, putting extra emphasis on certain beats that align with her steps, reminding her when to take higher, slightly longer steps.

Behind me, I assume the others make their own way. The armed men take up the rear, ensuring no one falls behind. With my goggles on, I have the luxury of being able to watch where I step.

Three

I sit in a corner of the shelter- huddled, chilled, and afraid. My fears are those of a child: unending dark and demons that scuttle about in the shadows feasting with wide, dog-like jaws on those who are alone. Like me. There is a pressing panic filling my lungs, suffocating the already thick air. Why is there no one here?

I am small and my grandfather is dead. I can still smell his death. I can hear my mother arguing with him, even in the afterlife. I can feel the wind that killed my father and my sister, whipping at my jean jacket. And, yet, there is nothing. Everything around me is far away and close at the same time. I am empty in the vast void. There is a whole wide world of nothing and anything. Potential terrors and waking dreams of memories flood around me. And I am so cold, wrapped around myself, surrounded by cold ghosts.

There are footsteps at the doorway. At the sound, an instantaneous relief, the demons flee. Someone enters and I break down in heavy breaths. The intruder drops something heavy and approaches. I recoil and, against my wishes, cry out a little.

"What's wrong, Little Owl?" Friend is there, I'm in his arms.

When I wake, I am alone. The man with the sunglasses stands watch, although it is mostly for show. If anyone did choose to attack us, we'd be pretty defenseless. With only a single lantern at his feet, there's no way we'd see anyone coming. We would be dead before anyone could draw any hidden weapons, if anyone in this little band actually has any.

"Can't sleep?" The man with the sunglasses has a gentle voice. I wonder if he was once a father. Since he knows I'm awake, there is no reason not to stand up and go talk to him while the others remain asleep.

"How could you tell I was awake?" I ask as I wrap a quilt from the cart around my shoulders and tiptoe around Red-hair and the man with the trench coat.

"Your breathing changed." His response is a verbal shrug. Of course, how else does anyone know someone's woken up?

"You can hear that from over here?"

"There's not much else to hear down here. Besides, when you're blind as long as I have been, your body decides to adjust its other senses." There is no pity or reluctance in his voice, just a deep-set resignation and apathy. I want to ask him what happened. Was he able to see before everything happened, before we fled underground? Or had he been born blind? And the question that was really on my mind: did blindness make him less afraid of the darkness down here?

I do not ask him. Once again, silence wins out over curiosity. Once again, all that's left is a waiting game. I hate waiting.

I do not know how long we sit there, the blind man and the girl mummified in her blanket, watching for demons that have never been successfully stopped. Out of the blue, there is a hand on my shoulder. The blind man jumps at the sound of my gasp. The old woman stands behind us, absent enough of every human quality that even our guard's heightened senses could not predict her coming.

"It's alright, Sights," she says to him in a motherly way, "I'll take the watch. I want to talk to our new recruit."

Sights, the ironically named blind man, walks to the place where I assume the old woman had been sleeping and lies down with his gun beside him and his glasses still covering his eyes. I listen, trying to hear his breathing pattern, but it is lost to me. Instead, the old woman's whispers find me.

"I know you do not want to address this, Songbird, but we have to trust each other if we are to get through this journey. All of us. I wish to tell you the stories of your companions and I wish to know yours."

I don't really know what to say. It isn't an unreasonable request, seeing as we are all living together now and will likely die together. If anyone is to remember any of us, it will be the others of our group. Still. There are memories I have laid to rest for a reason. I have never told my story before, never even admitted it aloud to myself. All I've been through, every heartbreak and loss seems far away- as long as I do not bring the ghosts back to life.

"I will start." Says the old woman softly. "Of course, you know my story. It isn't unusual. I survived the storms and came underground with the rest. I came with my sister, Amelia, who died with her husband, Jed, in the hospital attack. My two brothers and their families lived in another city, and I do not know what happened to them. After Amelia died, I met up with my first sojourning group, a band of four young adults who were determined to make their way to the surface to start again.

"We met on Platform 6. The Thunderbourne had just attacked the hospitals. Everyone came out into the streets, panicked, and I could not stand the screaming… I remember so vividly the screaming… so I ran away to Platform 6, which was the first platform outside our camp. The four were there, fierce and ready to storm the town, to raid it for supplies. Starving, they were thieves designed by desperation. Looking back, I don't know how I ever convinced them to even let me live, let alone travel with them. We became a small family, searching the tunnels for weeks before finding a way out. Three of us made it out. Sarah fell behind and never caught up. I stayed below, to lead other groups.

"Since then, I've led five other groups to the Surface. Only one has ever been… unsuccessful. It was the group right before yours and it fell apart because, of the seven travelers, only three ever talked to each other. Suspicions arose between two individuals, spreading disagreements and accusations like wildfire, and before we knew what had happened, one of the men open-fired on the group. He killed four of us, then killed himself.

"Wander and Sights were our two survivors. The rest of their stories even I don't know. They have been through more than they care to say, but they want to see the journey through to the end so I will take them."

The old woman looks my way expectantly. She expects me to ask her questions, she wants me to request elaboration. I do not understand why she is so insistent that I am interested in the names and backgrounds of my companions. I trust the old woman. I really have nothing to lose trusting any of them, but to learn their names, their stories, to become friends with them is cruel.

There is no ending to this journey where we end up together. We will most likely all die, here, in a ready-made tomb at the hands of creatures who crawled out of hell itself. Even if we make it to the surface, does she think we'll stay together? In what fairy-tale version of this life do we get to keep each other?

She takes my silence as an invitation to continue with the storytelling. She tells me how Red, the woman with the zebra-print earmuffs, suffers from seasonal depression and spent the majority of our time underground cutting herself with a shard of green glass she found in a garbage can on Platform 4. The old woman produces said shard, recalling how Red gave it to her, pleading with her to take her back to the sun, where she could become sane again.

Hunter, the trench coat man, had a dog with him when everyone fled underground. He had raised the dog from a puppy and it was an expensive, pure-bred genuine hunting dog. They wouldn't let any animals underground, so he tried to turn the dog loose. It sat there, howling as its master shut the station door, locking the dog outside in the storm. Since then, he has lost several friends and seen more deaths than he cares to count. Yet it is the dog, sitting there, waiting for his return, that drives him on to the surface.

The one-armed man, Soldier, lost his arm in exactly the way one would think with a title like his. An unrecognized civilian war hero with a backwards story: while serving overseas, Soldier received a little note that his family had gone missing after a freak wind storm hit his hometown. He went to investigate and joined the fleeing masses. His family is still M.I.A.

The mother and child joined the upward gang at Platform 14. The mother is a doctor, who overslept the day of the hospital attacks, accidentally surviving the massacre. She had the honor of watching the families of all her dead doctor-friends die of a sickness she couldn't cure. The latest outbreak gave her cause to flee with her son, trying to find somewhere, anywhere, with access to medicine. She can't stand the idea that her son could get sick and she wouldn't be able to save him.

The other woman, Tale, was a religious woman before everything. She had a husband, five children, parents, and a whole extended family- three siblings all with families and a mess of in- laws- who all passed away in storms and sickness and shadows. She keeps a photo album with her at all times, which is the treasure she clung to when I first saw her. It has a few pages of an old Bible in it as well as the pictures, which she uses for comfort and hope, though there is never enough light to read or see them. All she can do is hold them until she reaches a place filled with light.

Somewhere between howling dogs, festering wounds, and broken families, I get invested. The old woman's storytelling is upsettingly effective. I don't want to care for these individuals. My thoughts catch in my throat, a painful mass of regret and hesitation and deeply-embedded empathy. I stare at the old woman. I want to rip off the goggles and go blind. I never want to see another human being again. I cannot abide the way I want to cling to absolutely everyone. How badly I wish there was no such thing as letting go.

"And you, songbird?" The old woman prompts. "What is your story?"

I am upset. I do not want to tell her anything. I do not want to be vulnerable. I refuse to be. I never agreed to this. I never agreed to tell her my story. I have no wish to manipulate her the way she's manipulated me- to bind her to me and force her to care about whether I live or die. Let her forget about me. Let the whole world be spared the heartache of knowing me and watching me die!

"My parents are both dead." I say quickly, getting it over with. The sooner the better. Then we can move on and leave the dead where we've buried them. "I had a sister and a grandfather. They're gone too. And Friend…" Even without a proper name, he clings to my voice box and lingers in my eyes, disarming me completely. I can't finish my pathetic excuse of a story. I don't need to. The old woman knows.

"You can't walk away from loss." The old woman mothers, "It will always catch up with you."

"What do I do with it then?" I snap back, releasing a biting sob in the hollow of my chest.

"You let it be and take comfort in the fact that loss means you have loved and loved well. You are better, stronger, for the hardships you bear."

I stand and walk away, unable to take the mad woman's bullshit anymore.

Four

It is Sights who comes for me. I am sitting with my grandfather's night vision goggles clenched in a fist and my face so forcefully pressed against my knees I think maybe I do want to make myself blind after all. I'm far enough away that the echoes of my sighing, surviving breaths cannot betray me to the company, although I'm sure Sights hears. I'm sure that's why he comes.

Sights, being the strong, silent type, does not say a word. I only know he's there because I've been nervously looking up every so often, predicting in hope or fear that someone would be there. He has brought the lantern, a token that he does not want to frighten me. He wants me to know he's there, even with my knees drawn to my chin. There would be no other reason a blind man would bring a lantern.

Ugh. I'm a predictable fool, with a predictable, foolish heart. It means more than I care to admit that he's here. He's not my hero. I can't talk to him, I can't interact with him, I just can't. He's not my hero.

He just stands there, watching me. Well, not watching me. He stands there, listening to me as I let out the most private, revealing breaths I've ever taken. Air from somewhere deeper than my lungs, somewhere more secret, more fragile, tears through me and escapes into the darkness.

This is the most hated version of me I've ever known. I cannot cry, but it feels like I cannot stop crying. I'm alone with no way to let anyone in, despite someone standing not three feet away who could help me. No. There are no heroes here. All the heroes are dead. All my heroes are dead.

My legs fall asleep. My breath slows and my swollen eyes are weary. I've spent all my strength just sitting here. It isn't fair to any of them, the others, who are waiting for me to get my shit together and continue on our way. The thought of them dying because I can't come to terms with the others who are already dead brings me to my feet.

It will be a rough trek, this wake-span, but I will do what I must. The old woman's stories have served their purpose. I go back with Sights. He puts an arm around my shoulder, supporting me as we go. I'm surprised I allow him that familiarity, yet I do. As we walk, I hold the lantern, he holds the gun.

Everyone except Red is up and waiting to move out when we return to the camp. Apparently they always let Red sleep until the last possible moment. She is always the last to fall asleep and the last to wake. When the old woman shines a flashlight at us and sees that we are returning, she wakes Red, who moans and struggles with summoning the will to live.

I linger near Sights as we trudge on, but he does not support me or speak with me. I am grateful for his silence. Being so long without proper communication leaves me somewhat lacking in forced social situations. I wonder how many before us have taken these same silent steps.

Red has started humming again. It's a song I've heard before, though I can't place it. I fall in step with her and join her humming. She thinks I'm mocking her and shoots me a deadly look, tripping because she's not paying attention. I catch her, ask if she's alright. She pulls away, muttering about how fine she is. Trying to fix something I've inadvertently broken, I ask what it was she was singing.

"I know the tune, I think, but I can't remember what it is."

She shrugs, shutting herself away.

"Shalom Chaverim." Wander contributes behind us. He sees that he has taken us off guard. "It's an old Israeli song, usually sung in a round?"

"Do you remember the words?" I ask.

A hush falls over the group, even quieter than the unspeakable silence of before. It's as if everyone quiets their steps, their breaths, even their thoughts in anticipation of this. Wander obliges us by starting the song. His deep voice turns into a gorgeous, obviously trained and talented bass with just the right amount of rumble.

"Shalom chaverim, Shalom chaverim!
Shalom! Shalom!
L'hitraot, L'hitraot.
Shalom! Shalom!"

By the second verse, Red has remembered the words and joins in, quietly adding her wistful voice like a breath upon the pulse of the song.

"Shalom chaverim, Shalom chaverim!
Shalom! Shalom!
'Till we meet again, 'till we meet again
Shalom! Shalom!"

Soon all of us are chanting or humming the song. It really does help when trying to remember when and how to step over the tracks and makes our journey a little cheerier. I pause a moment, listening to the voices of my companions, and remember learning about sailors who, in days long gone, would sing together as they rowed their boats to keep rhythm and pass time when only the endless waves stretched out before them. With the dark expanse of tracks before and behind us, and the fear of storms driving us onward, we aren't so different from those sailors.

The next sleep-span, there is some chatter amongst those who are not as tired as the others- a lingering ease from the singing. Despite the tiresome start, I am not as sleepy as perhaps I should be. I look around, noticing that Tale is up as well, running her fingers along the outside of her album. I set up my bed mat beside hers and offer her my night-vision goggles.

"I can't guarantee you'll be able to see anything, but if you want to try, you're welcome to."

She can't use the flashlights, they are only for back up if the lantern dies and the lantern itself does not give out enough light to allow for reading. She eagerly takes the goggles, puts them on, opens her book, and is absorbed in its contents. I lie down, turning away from her to allow her the privacy of a personal moment.

I wake a little later as Tale, trying so very hard not to wake me, places my goggles next to my hand and withdraws. Feeling a little like Sights, I can hear a telling raggedness in her breath, which lulls as her breathing slows. She sleeps.

The next wake-span, as we eat our breakfast from the well-stocked store-cart that Hunter pulls (sometimes with the help of Solider). The child,

Hugs, asks if I know any other songs we could sing. I try another round, humming it because, once again, the words escape me. To my delight, the little boy knows the song.

"I learned it in Sunday School!" he declares. The boy can't be old enough to remember anything from his Surface life, so I guess some other settlements were more civilized than the one my mother, grandfather, and I were at. What would a camp be like with proper church services and Sunday School?

"Do you remember the words, honey?" His mother prompts. Beaming, the boy sings with a confident shout.

"Love, love, love, love
the gospel in one word is love
love your neighbor as your brother
God loves all!"

"Oh!" Joins in Soldier. "I've heard that tune. Joyce used to sing that all the time. Different words, though. Let's see... Uh, something about roses..."

The song comes flooding back to me and I'm sent reeling in the memory of Friend, who taught it to me. As I hear Friend's voice in my heart, I whisper the song in the dark.

"Rose rose rose red
Will I ever see thee wed?

I will marry at thy will, sire,
at thy will."

Soldier nods vigorously. "That's the one!
Only… did you say 'I will marry at <u>thy</u> will'? I've
always heard it 'at <u>my</u> will'. It changes the entire
meaning of the song, doesn't it?"

Hugs pouts because we've abandoned his
version. Tale softly suggests that, since our versions
are different and it changes the meaning completely,
maybe we should use the Sunday School words as
we walk. At this, Hugs beams and starts us out. The
more we sing, the more verses the boy remembers,
until we are all sure he is making them up as we go
along. None of us, however, have the heart to tell
him off, since he is so happy. Eventually, we all
drop out of the song except Hugs, who continues to
hum happily to himself.

Suddenly, we stop. Red, who has slowed her
pace and dropped behind everyone except Wander
and Sights, is huddled in a ball on the dirty tracks.
She is not moving or making any noise.

"Wait a moment." The old woman says and
everyone halts.

"No." Red whispers, void of any and all
emotion. "Keep going. Finish your quest. Don't
wait for me; I'm going to die here in the darkness."

Mother directs Hugs away, distracting him with a game they've often played together before. Everyone looks to see what the old woman will do.

"Nonsense." She says "We aren't going anywhere without you. This is the depression talking."

"I know, but what do I do?" she whispers, her voice raising in pitch and tension as panic shows itself from behind her apathetic composure. "There's nothing anywhere. Everything is gone and I'll be gone too, soon enough. I can't breathe here. The darkness chokes me. I can't, I just can't."

Tale approaches, carefully dropping her photo album along the way. She kneels down beside Red, between the broken woman and the old storyteller. Tale twists a bright curl around her finger, tucking it behind Red's ear.

"That's why we're doing this, Sweetie." Tale soothes, "The darkness is choking all of us, but there's a land of light waiting for us. Where the wind still sweeps across the prairie and birds still greet the dewy spring. We're going to get there, all of us, even if we have to go through hell itself. Every time you take a step, you are crushing the shadows that haunt you. You are brave, Rachel, brave enough to face the darkness and seek the light."

Tale leans over and kisses Red on the forehead and, in a voice meant only for the two of them, says, "Come on, lady. We'll face this together. We will see sunshine together."

Red manages to sit up. Tale helps her to her feet. Holding on to each other for dear life, the women begin to walk to the supplies cart. Tale and the old woman get Red something to eat and drink, and a piece of cloth to wash her face.

I look around at the rest of the group, trying to make sense of some of the details of our dynamic. Hunter has joined Mother's and Hugs' game. He has Hugs laughing hysterically on the ground as he pretends to be a tickle monster. Soldier and Wander are talking to each other about how far they think we've traveled and what platform should be coming next. Sights is characteristically quiet, head tilted ever so slightly, listening.

No one seems put off by what has just taken place. I follow the lantern light to the one who holds it. I don't want to interrupt him, but Sights is the only one not invested in someone at the moment, so I talk to him.

"Why not let Red carry a light for a while so she doesn't feel so dark?"

Sights shakes his head. "We've tried it. Gave her a flashlight early on in this venture. She ran down the batteries just staring into it. Wouldn't move or talk or anything. Since then we've had one lantern and one lantern only, and I carry it."

I try to imagine the scene. How much must one yearn for light before they become so desperate that, once they have it, they refuse to look away? Recalling the days of darkness right before my grandfather passed, I understand. My insides knot together. Humans are not meant to live this way. We have to get to the surface, and soon!

Five

I think, if we were to let them, Soldier and Wander would eat all our supplies in one sitting. They have already consumed twice the rations everyone else has and, because of it, neither of them are allowed near the cart for any reason. Wander is one of the gunmen so he mostly stay towards the back of the group anyway, Soldier by his side. They spend a great deal of time trying to sneak up on one another and scare each other.

Hunter watches over Hugs and his mother. The three are like a family. When Hugs gets fussy, Hunter lets him ride in the cart. He's little enough that it doesn't add too much weight and sometimes Hunter rushes, causing him to squeal in delight. This makes the old woman smile to herself.

Red and Tale, Wander and Soldier, Hunter and Mother and Hugs… I wonder what kept me from seeing the inner workings of this group before. The old woman who leads us all, Sights who follows behind and protects us all. And who am I? Where do I belong?

The trail is different here. We are no longer on tracks; we're in a tunnel that was made after the storms started- when it became apparent that the subways would be key to humanity's survival. It is darker, somehow, and smells of earth and moisture. A natural smell, one that lulls me into the memory of something I can't quite reach. I feel full of something old and I want to sleep.

For a moment, I think there may be a forest around us; a thick, luscious forest from a dream I once had. I believe I can see starlight amongst the branches. Warm, green stars welcoming me into the shadows of the trees, whose trunks are open to embrace me. The sky floods upon me like I'm in melted chocolate that is just cool enough to eat without getting burned.

"Hugs," I call out lazily as I turn, ready to ask him if he's ever had chocolate before. That's when I see the stars for what they really are.

There must be hundreds of Thunderbourne watching us from the path we have just taken, slowly inching towards us. They are above us as well, looking down, and some come up from the ground below us. We cannot see any part of their form, for they are formless as far as anyone knows. They are so fully veiled in darkness, that only their eyes can ever be seen, green as lightning that strikes too close and never blinking.

A piercing gunshot resounds near my ear. The ringing that follows sounds like an eerie chorus of bells tolling something terrible. For a moment, I panic, and think I am blind and lost. I scream out titles where names should have come forth, like I am calling them back to me:

"Old woman! Sights! Mother!"

And I cry out for people who haven't existed for years, whom I never got a chance to warn against their doom. Perhaps I think I can do so now, as my doom approaches.

"Daddy! Grampa! Mommy! Jenna!"

In the midst of my own voice, another someone fights the silence and the screaming. It is the old woman.

"Songbird." She commands in a calm voice, "Come away now."

Something is moving my feet. I run instinctively, like a light-footed deer. Or, perhaps, the trees are running around me, and I am standing quite still next to a shimmering stream. Where are all these surface images coming from? Some form trips in front of me. It is Red.

"Rachel!" I whisper urgently and, perhaps, a little too loudly for it to actually be considered a whisper, "Get up!"

We run until we spend all our panicked adrenaline. We are all accounted for, but badly shaken. The boy cannot stop crying, but will not be held even by his mother. The supplies are half gone, spilled along the way. Our eyes search each other, wordlessly asking every important question: how much longer can we go on? What happens now? What do we do?

Sights digs deep into the cart and produces what could be the last of the flashlights. It flickers on and we all gather a little closer to the light, which reveals a cesspool of unimaginable source and stench surrounding us. We all recoil from each other, although none of us has energy enough to panic again, even to escape the sludge.

"Onward." The old woman says through clenched teeth, as if she's never been here before.

We march on. We march for what should have been many days, but since the sun has long since abandoned our pathetic world, we march on for one long, hellish night. The flashlight goes out and Red screams for an age while Tale tries to find her in the utter darkness. When the light leaves us, we see clearly that the Thunderbourne are following us on either side of the tracks where subway lines are abandoned and unkempt.

We follow the railroad because it is our hope for a miracle. The Thunderbourne do not go near the tracks or any of the platforms, though we do not know why, and so the railroad becomes a symbol of an exodus out of the land of the dead. We stop to rest only at platforms. Those who cannot make it that far rest in the cart and we pull them as far as we can before we wake them.

The glowing green eyes march on by our side far enough into the darkness that our guns would be useless, if guns are even useful against the Thunderbourne. None of us know for sure, as we don't know what keeps them away, and all of us sense that if we were to open fire, they would attack.

So we march ever onwards, ever, hopefully, upwards. The last of the supplies are consumed in silence on Platform 23. There are no groups at this meal; we all eat alone in the tightest knit group we can make. When it is time to rest, Sights stands guard and the old woman takes my hand, signing for silence. She brings me away from the refugees, to the edge of the platform's magic where the fierce lightning eyes begin to gather around us, hungering for something sinister.

The old woman does not acknowledge the otherworldly stares. Whether she sees them or not, I do not know. But I see them and, for the first time, notice that although their eyes are green, it is a different green than I've ever seen before through the goggles. Also, despite having the goggles, I cannot see them any clearer than my own eyes would be able to see them. I am chilled at the realization.

"Time is running out." The old woman brings me back from the fear, back to the dirty darkness of the tunnels. Her voice has a strange tone that leaves no room for questioning how she knows what she does. Her eyes are soft, but sure. Wander told me that once they were the color of the sea, with the same vast power. Today I think they would be gray, with the energy of a gathering storm.

I think she is talking about the supplies, but she looks around and I realize her concern is more immediate than starvation. "Every day they dare to come nearer. We must be ready."

I grip the faithful knife at my hip. It helped my grandfather through many hard times, against many foes. Still, I wonder if it is ready to face the foes ahead.

"I am ready." I say, surprising myself with how unwavering my voice sounds even as it echoes through the tunnel.

"You are a woman with the strength to survive all of this," the old woman continues in her strange certainty ,"but if you do survive, you will be alone. The last of the living in this land."

As she leaves, back to her family of refugees, I think I hear the sharp intake and the slow exhale of weeping breaths. My heart pounds with choice, fear, and determination. I think about the people who are all about to die. My hand, clutched to the bone handle of my ancestor's weapon, lingers to strike at the darkness.

I want Red to see the sun. I want Tale to read her sacred stories one last time. I want Wander and Soldier to go on to many more adventures together. I want Hunter to marry Mother and find a puppy to keep Hugs company as he sings all the songs of Sunday School and is able to finally understand the imagery behind the lyrics. I want Sights to feel the warmth of the dawn and the softness of the wind- to repay all the beauty he will never see. I want the old woman to lead everyone back to the surface, where life can begin again. I want Grandfather to have nowhere to hide his despair. I want mommy to bandage my scraped knees and give me mints to calm my upset stomach. I want to wake up to daddy singing obnoxiously on a Sunday and my sister snuggled beside me on the cold winter nights.

As I stand there, reminiscing, I realize my wishes are lost on dead men. I have to move on; I have to let them go. I have to block their screaming from my ears as I continue this journey alone. My knife goes to its home at my hip. I try to comfort myself with the fact that no one will see me sneak away. My betrayal will never be known to them.

I slip off the platform edge, onto the tracks below. The surface is uneven and little pebbles and pieces of fossilized garbage are kicked up with every step. I can hear the far away whimpering of Hugs as he slips into slumber and his mother whispering a lullaby.

They are safe for now. Something inside me releases. It would be so easy to just go back to them... to find a place among their footsteps and laughter again... to protect them when the time comes. To die with them.

No. I'm not ready to face that path to certain mortality. Or, more likely, I am not ready to watch them all die. I creep on in the pebbles instead, sideways, with my hands always on the platform drop-wall, to make sure I do not wander off into the wild earth again.

"Are you leaving us, Songbird?"

The voice, so near, so hurt, startles me. I jump back with a small cry. Of course he is here, standing faithful watch as ever, hearing every single sound. Stupid to think I could slip by without him hearing me. The guardian angel of our group. Yea though I walk...

"Quick, Sights, pull me up!"

I can't force myself to make confession to my crime, maybe I wanted to be caught all along, so I begin to fabricate a story involving me going for a walk, falling off the platform, and being unable to get back to the group. Sights helps me up and listens to my story. He doesn't ask why I didn't call out for help or what I was doing out for a walk, so I am sure he has called my bluff. He only nods towards the group.

"Get some rest." He says, and I know he means to listen for my slowing breath. I oblige eventually. Apparently the girl tucked into a mat, who closes her eyes of her own accord, will always fall asleep before the blind man with a gun who is carefully keeping watch.

I am exhausted when I wake, despite sleeping past everyone except Red. We have apparently decided to leave the cart and mats behind, travel as lightly as possible and as quickly as possible. The old woman says we might have two days or so left to travel, as best as she can tell. Since we have no food and the Thunderbourne are getting closer far more quickly than anyone would like, we just have to press on and support each other as much as we can.

As we travel, the old woman develops a habit of watching me out of the disappointed, and strangely compassionate, corner of her eye. I do not meet her gaze, not that she'd see it, but walk in silence somewhere near Sights. It is not until well past the moment the old woman stops turning her head back to me that I realize I've overlooked a detail: two more days to travel. So the old woman was keeping track of time.

Six

I don't know why this detail haunts me. There is no reason why the fact that the old woman had secretly been keeping a record of time should make me so upset and hopeful. The old woman lied to us or, at the very least, did not fully tell us the truth. She kept something very human away from us when we needed most to remain human. She may as well have kept songs or food or dreaming from us.

On the other hand, time exists again! If time can remain alive, though unseen, in the very bowels of the earth, maybe humans can too. Maybe there is hope of a life on the Surface after all...

Just as I wonder, something sparkles up ahead. I remove my goggles, and the glimmering hope stays actualized. There are many tiny lights ahead and not a single one of them are the ghostly green that haunts our fears. They shimmer white, sometimes gold, and glorious. Together, they shine to illuminate the pathway. Such a gathering of light has never been seen underground.

"What is it?" queries Sights, who has heard the collective intake and hold of our breath.

"It's light." I reply so very softly as to not damage the sacredness of the moment. Red lets out a cry that is halfway between a shriek and a gasp and takes off in a mad rush towards the miracle.

Everyone reaches out to try and stop her, but she is slight and most everyone is blind, so she eludes us. We run after her, towards the light. First Tale and Soldier, who are the quickest of us all, then me, Mother, Hunter (who is holding Hugs), and Wander, whose gun is at the ready. The old woman and Sights are at the back, walking quickly behind us, but unable to run.

We lose Rachel right away. I remember hearing somewhere that people who are depressed are encouraged to pick up sports or athletic pastimes. I wonder if Red was a runner in her old life. If we were on the surface, I bet she would be begging Tale to go run with her every morning. I bet Red would have no trouble getting up with the sun and, roles reversed, I can just picture her trying to coax Tale out of bed.

The light is coming from around a bend. Everyone hesitates before proceeding into a world they have been waiting a lifetime to see. The light is overwhelming, brilliant beyond our wildest imagination! The whole tunnel, as far as we can see, is illuminated with candles.

There must be thousands of candles, each one set in a little house-shaped platform built into the wall, burning with courageous luster. It is mystifying. Who placed these here? Who tends them? What keeps them all burning? I've never even seen this many candles. How can there possibly be enough in the world to replace and replenish those dark spots when a candle has melted?

"There." Someone breathes, barely audibly. Then I see her. Her hair, loose, long, and gleaming, holding her earmuffs instead of wearing them, her long, teal coat worn and ripped in several places and falling off one shoulder, Rachel walks slowly through the tunnel, trailing her right hand against a wall. Her chin is lifted high, toward the candles, and her eyes are closed. She looks like a ghost.

We just stand there. This place seems too special to enter, like a strange afterlife, yet we cannot take our eyes off our strange, sad apparition. Red drops her earmuffs and covers her face with the now-empty hand. Suddenly, she folds over on herself, like a paper being crumpled and thrown away, and weeps.

That is enough. Tale slips through our group, handing her photo album to Soldier, and walks down the tunnel. I see, for the first time, how beautiful Tale is. She has dark, straight hair that stops just below her shoulders. She wears dark gray stockings under a black skirt, slightly scuffed shoes, and a cream button-up-the front shirt underneath a maroon sweater. She has a gray scarf as well, but no coat, and I wonder if she's always walked with that tense shiver in her shoulders and fingertips.

I look at the others. What else have I missed? What have the shadows hidden from me about them? Soldier holds Tale's book against his forest green jacket, which has survived well, much in the same way that Tale would have held it. He is wearing tan cargo-style pants and military boots much like my grandfather's. There is a knife hidden in the left boot, where his arm can easily reach it. He is lighter than I initially thought, in every way possible: light pale skin, golden hair that, along with his facial hair, gives him the look of a lion. Only his eyes are dark, chocolate-colored and shadowed by deep-set features.

Mother looks older than I remember. Her sandy blonde hair is clearly beginning to gray to match her weary-set eyes. She looks weak and ill-nourished and her clothes reveal that she has lost some weight recently. Her pants are belted to keep them up and her sweatshirt is baggy, but looks the warmer for it. There is a horse embroidered on the shirt, looking out from underneath a quilted gray jacket.

Her son is a picture of neglect that breaks my heart. His jeans and tee-shirt are ridiculously small for him. A scarf of salmon shade is wrapped around his shoulders, arms, and waist; an attempted make-shift coat under his actual coat. There are mittens clipped to his coat sleeves, though he doesn't wear them. He has no shoes, only socks, layered together to protect his feet and keep them warm. I suppose he outgrew the shoes he wore setting out on this journey. That must be why someone is almost always carrying him. Any shard of glass or sharp rock would injure him almost immediately.

Hugs clings to Hunter, burying his face into the crevice where Hunter's neck met his strong shoulder. Hunter is dark-featured, but with cream-colored skin and full lips. He is bearded and his black hair is long and wavy. His trench coat fits him almost perfectly, despite his time wandering. I wonder if the coat was tight on him before, and he has lost the exact perfect amount of weight while traveling, or if it has always fit him and he's been doing fine wandering the tunnels.

Wander surprises me the most. He is ginger, like Red, but in a more cinnamon-in-your-coffee kind of way. His face is splattered with freckles, like some artist got frustrated with his pale complexion and tried to scold him with a brush that had rosy paint on it. His eyes are copper and bright, despite the way the rest of him seems to have sunken in a bit. His clothes are also more raggedy than the rest of ours, hastily patched in places, and all in a rainbow of dull, dirty colors. His facial hair is short and uneven, signs that he still tries to keep it trimmed, though I cannot imagine how he attempts to do so.

Wander, of course, is holding his gun. I know absolutely nothing about guns, though the one he holds looks to be a rifle of some kind. It is beautiful, for all it is meant to kill, with a wooden finish that reminds me of the guitars some men carry. I wonder if this gun has a name. She deserves a name.

Sights carries a gun as well, though it is somewhat more battered than Wander's. I never really noticed just how big Sights is. He is huge and broad, with light umber skin and dark brown hair that hangs in a braid to the small of his back. He stands so still as if, despite his blindness, he can see that this is a place deserving respect. He has no facial hair to speak of and wears soft, brown pants and a light gray shirt underneath a bomber-style brown leather jacket. He is wearing cowboy boots. Real, legit, cowboy boots. At one time, I thought that I looked the most out of place in our group. Now, I'm sure it is Sights.

"Ma'am." Sights says as I look him over. I blush before I realize that he's talking to the old woman. "I think we should keep moving."

His voice breaks whatever spell held us in place. We continue walking through the illumination of mismatched candles. The warmth of the tiny fires flickers on our skin. Soon it is very hard to keep awake. It feels safe here, warm and inviting. It feels like we've walked into comfort again where slumber could actually be restful instead of the terror-filled, fitful sleep-spans we experienced in the dark.

The darkness feels far away, although we have not been long in the light. It seems forever ago, now that we are out of it. Of course, there's no real way of knowing whether or not we've seen the last of our lightless days, but we can see no end of our friends the candles.

Hugs pokes his little face out for a while, staring at the world with big blue eyes. He has to constantly push his brown curls out of his face as he takes in the world around him. I see him smile for the first time. He is going to break hearts some day.

By the time we reach Red, everyone is a little more relaxed. Tale has calmed Red down, and we are all ready to move on happily. The walk is pleasant. We chatter and laugh and hum little fragmented songs. The longer we keep going, however, the harder it gets not to remember that there is no food or time to rest. There isn't even water here and, in the light, no one can see any Thunderbourne. We do not know if that is because there are no Thunderbourne here or if the light hides the only feature we can see of them, their eyes.

When Hugs begins to cry, I fish around in my backpack and find a few granola bars and a bottle of water at the bottom. I give him part of a granola bar, slipping it to him with a finger over my mouth so he knows it is our little secret. No one can know that I have food. I do not want to risk an uprising against each other when things get really bad.

I know the temptations of these kinds of days, how the stomach aches in anticipation of starvation. I know how shaking fingers grab at every last morsel of food, panicking, when you know tomorrow there will be nothing. This group cannot afford the luxury of panic. I will keep these supplies for Hugs. Everyone else will just have to suck it up and starve until we get to the surface.

As we travel on, the candles get thicker until we've all shed our coats and sweaters, draping them on our arms or tying them at our waists. As hard as it is to imagine, we get tired of the luminescent tunnel very quickly. It is hot and we are tired and hungry and irritable. We stop laughing and fall into quarreling.

I carry Hugs, sometimes, holding him on my hip and feeding him bites of granola. It gives Mother and Hunter a chance to be alone. She leans on him sometimes. She lets him give her strength so long as she does not need to demonstrate bravery for her son. When we stop for short breaks, he crumples his trench coat up in his lap and she puts her head there. He plays with her hair and there is a bittersweet smile that plays at the corner of his mouth.

Tale shows Red her pictures, naming family member after family member and reading her passages of scripture. Soldier and Wander sleep and bicker. Who knew that men without food got so explosive and, yet, at the same time, have no energy at all? The old woman sings to herself and Sights just sits off by himself, still and distant. He might be meditating.

At least they have some comfort. Prayers, meditation, candlelight, treats, songs, and sleep. At least they can take comfort in some small pleasures as starvation and shadows compete to kill them. *And you?* A small voice whispers. *Have you resigned yourself to outlive them already? Are you ready to sacrifice them for your own solitary survival? Are you not one of them?*

I look around at the raggle-taggle group. These are people. Actual people sit next to me. It's been so long since I've been aware of the presence of actual, living human beings near me. I see them more clearly as we sit in light and in such a dire situation. They are souls, or whatever it is that perpetuates life, intellect, and creativity- everything that separates us from plants and animals.

So far as we know, the plants and animals are gone. So maybe the will to survive, the ability to give up what makes us human when absolutely necessary, is what makes us actually human. If that is the case, am I more or less human for being willing to passively murder everyone around me? Am I a monster or is this a new start for humanity?

I turn my back on the group, take a small sip of water, and we move out. I strap my backpack on Hugs and lift him up, giving him a piggy-back ride. Mother smiles at me and mouths a silent "thank you." There's a child on my back. There's a child who is going to die on my back, and so, there is a wiggling, talking, laughing corpse on my back.

The thought of this almost makes me dump him off my back. I recognize that I am not doing well mentally. I am not dealing with this well. The old woman's words haunt me and I feel like a killer. I wish I could forget about everything. I wish I could get drunk and sleep for a really, really long time. My eyes hurt from the brightness of the tunnel and the dammed up tears behind them.

I close my eyes for a few moments and, when I open them, I stop short. My heart lunges. Wander gives a little, falling breath. The safety of the candles is fading. There is darkness up ahead.

"No!" Red's panic is contagious. "No, no, no, no, no!" She backs up, through the group, and we are all afraid that she is going to bolt again.

"Rachel…" The old woman soothes, reaching a hand out to help her. She shrinks away.

"Damn it!" Soldier hits the tunnel wall. Wander drops his arms to his side, accidentally letting part of his gun hit the ground.

Meanwhile, Red is hugging her knees to her chest, eyes clamped shut tightly, banging the back of her head against the wall. Tale, her usual comfort and strength, cannot tear herself away from the shock of the unavoidable darkness.

I make a mental note: two women rendered helpless by the sight of the next step in our journey, two men who are ready to kill the next thing that looks at them wrong, one of whom is already lashing out, the other also useless. So that leaves us with an old woman, a child, a mother, and a blind man.

And Hunter. Where is Hunter? I look around and see him. He has a revolver pointed at something down the tunnel from where we came. It's a shadow, no more than a shadow of a distorted form, and yet it makes my blood run cold. It stares at us with jade eyes.

Mother screams as another Thunderbourne crawls out of a candle platform, closer to us. Hunter pulls the trigger and the blast of the gun echoes all around us. The sound brings out seven more Thunderbourne from God-knows-where. Soldier produces a hand-held gun as well and shoots a round at the formless ones.

Of course, it does no good. As Sights and Wander raise their rifles, the old woman shouts at us to keep going, quickly. We do as we're told. All, that is, except Red, who cowers all the more into herself. Without thought, I pass Hugs to his mother and go back for Red.

"Rachel." I tell her as calmly as I can. "I know you're frightened, but we have to go. Now."

"I can't." She whispers back. "I can't do it. I can't. I can't."

I try to pull her to her feet and she slaps me hard across the face. I stumble back. The jolt has given me an idea.

"Wait!" I cry and run after Mother. "I need my pack!"

Mother all but rips the backpack off her son, breaking one of the straps to do so, and throws it at me and keeps running. I catch it and turn back to Red, searching frantically.

I scream as something comes up beside me! Then urge my heart to stop racing as I realize it is Sights. He fires his rifle at the shadows, to no real avail. My shaking fingers find what they were looking for. I silently slip my grandfather's night-vision goggles over Rachel's hair.

"These are your courage now. You will be able to see, even in the night." She looks me in the eye. She understands. I help her to her feet. She flicks the goggles over her eyes.

"Come on, Sights, let's go!" All three of us dash off together, rejoining our scattered party just in time to slip out of the candlelight and into heavy darkness.

Seven

I am not prepared for the severity of our situation. We stumble more than run through the subway tunnels. Everything works against us: the tracks which trip us, the blinding black air, the fatigue of restless wandering, the cramps of the starving... everything wants us dead.

There is no way of knowing where we are or who is nearby. I hear someone beside me, straining to breathe, but I have no idea who it is. The chaos is unbearable and a horrible part of me wishes I had left Red to die and kept my grandfather's goggles for myself. Partly because they were my grandfather's and I know that I will never get them back, but mostly because, without them, I am fighting the urge to give up and let the shadows take me.

I take a wrong step and trip, falling hard. Someone accidentally kicks my spine. The cursing that follows as he stumbles forward reveals him to be Soldier. His gun falls out of his hand as he stumbles, but I cannot hear him stop to retrieve it. As far as I can tell, he regains his balance and keeps going.

Well, if he's not going to… I feel around on my hands and knees for the gun, tearing apart my palms with pebbles and loose nails. It is risky to take these precious seconds, but another weapon would ease my mind a bit. I don't know how I'll use it, how I'll ever see enough to take aim at anything, but instinct says *take it* and I listen.

As soon as I have my fingers clenched around the handle, I leap up and keep running. My lungs feel explosive, my heart is the count-down. I am gasping for oxygen in this smog-filled shadowed land. All around me are flashes of eyes and the sensation that dark hands are reaching for me, that I am seconds away from becoming the playthings of demons.

I open my eyes as wide as I can, desperate for a way to locate my enemies and avoid my friends. There is no way to do so. I lose all sanity and scream out, firing shots at the surrounding Thunderbourne. I do not know if it helps or hinders me. I don't know anything anymore.

Somewhere before me, far in front of me, there is a flash of unearthly jade light. It lasts only a second, but it fills the tunnel with terror and the screams of one of my companions, a woman. Here is the explosion within me. I gasp and fall to my knees, grieving for each woman in our company in turn, because there is no way to tell who was just taken by the Thunderbourne.

The click in my hand informs me that I've just used my last bullet. The acknowledgment of that fact is delayed. I spend a few moments trying to fire an empty gun. Throwing it aside, I take out my grandfather's knife, reaching deep inside for the will to stand up again and fight. I stab out at an unnervingly close set of eyes. The creature does not react in pain, but slows a little.

Right behind me, another of my comrades screams. I imagine it is Wander. The hair on the back of my neck rises and the flash that follows consumes me. I am blinded and bombarded with sharp, tingling pain throughout my body. My ears ring and I'm sure that I scream as I fall forward.

I'm not sure how long I am caught in the ripples of the Thunderbourne attack. Long enough that, by the time it is over, I cannot move. I stay there, lying on the tracks, immobile and tearlessly weeping, sweating and shivering. Around me, eyes look at me and move past, leaving me to die for the pleasure of hunting my friends.

I count the screams as they happen, more from the quaking of the earth around me than from what I can actually hear of their pain. One: Soldier, going down fighting like he's never fought before. Two: Another woman, possibly Tale. I imagine her photo album left behind, lit on fire by the flash, burning into a precious pile of ashes. Three, Four, and Five: The only trio I can think of: Hugs, Mother, and Hunter. No doubt they went after Hugs first and, in a chain of events, Mother tried to help her son and Hunter tried to help her.

Who is left? I try to raise my head and find that I can, but barely. Not that it helps me survey the scene. I can't use my eyes. I forgot. I close them, so I stop trying to see, and recall who, if anyone, may still be alive. Wander, Soldier, Tale, Red, Mother, Hunter, Hugs: all dead. That leaves only the old woman and Sights. I can't imagine how either one would have made it. Yet, here I am. Alive. Despite it all.

The Thunderbourne must have let me go. There's no other explanation. Those terrors looked at me, saw that I was alive, and chose to leave me here. I think of what the old woman said to me on the last platform: "the last of the living in the land of the dead." What frightens me most is the thought of going on, not knowing if I will stumble upon the bodies of my friends. Or will I step very near to them, but never know it? Are their bodies even still there? Or are they lost forever, their only remains left in the green and yellow spots that dot my eyes from the flash?

I pull myself up to my knees. I can find no Thunderbourne around me, so I take the non-existent time to eat a granola bar and sip at my water. I need strength to carry me on. If I cannot have strength of heart, I must at least have physical strength. There are two granola bars left, some water, and not much else. My jacket is in my bag, along with the scarf that had been wrapped around Hugs, which he stuffed in my bag when the candles made it too hot for his comfort. I have nothing else, except my father's camera.

I move my neck in small rotations, trying to relax the muscles and prepare them for another unknowable stretch of this journey. Only, something plays at the back of my mind. I'm confused; turned around. I do not know which way I am supposed to go. One way will lead back to the tunnel of candles. However, not soon enough, perhaps, to allow me to correct my mistake and get to the surface. I only have the time span of two granola bars and half a bottle of water. I have no time for errors, yet no way of ensuring against them.

I put my grandfather's knife away and slip back into my jacket. I wrap the scarf around my neck and bury my face in the softness. It doesn't exactly smell like anything, but I miss little Hugs and having a part of him close to me helps. Throwing my pack over my neck and under one arm, I pick a direction and continue trudging through the darkness, hoping beyond hope that it leads me to the Surface.

My heart quivers painfully. I'm shaking in grief, which is nothing new to me. Once again, I've let my heart become attached to those I'm not meant to keep. And it isn't like it's a surprise. This was always the outcome. I always knew that I would be separated from them. The old woman even knew; didn't she say that everyone else would die and I would remain?

It is harder to actually walk the path of fate than to acknowledge it will someday come to pass. I wish my heart could just scar over already. I heard somewhere once that letting go is not painful; it is holding on, fighting, which brings about suffering. I know now that I would give up the hope of ever having a friend again if only I could be spared what I feel now, the cycle of goodbyes that I know will follow me to my end.

The eyes are back, but I can't bring myself to care. They follow me, watching me, keeping a good distance away. My head knows that if they take me, everything will have been a waste. I refuse to let this be a waste. There must be a payout in the end. I will hold all the souls of the fallen and, when I come to the surface, I will release them to the wind and the sun, where they can be at peace. I will not, however, let their souls be trapped here. I have to get them home.

I walk until I cannot. My spine feels like it is about to split open, my head is pounding with every pulse of my heart. I drop to my knees, throwing off my pack, which I use as a pillow. All the fear in the world cannot keep my eyelids from closing.

Eight

Darkness to darkness, I awake. I am confused at first, wondering why I cannot see, wondering which way I must go, wondering why it feels like there is nothing warm left in the world. When I remember, I go on.

Despite the heartache, I am proud that I have gotten this far. There is something particularly rewarding about knowing that you have every reason to lie down and give up, and yet you go on anyway. There may be nothing left to live for, but I'm living anyway. Damn you, despair, you shall not have me! I swear I shall fight you and death with every step that I have left in me! You may not have me.

To drive my point home, I flip off the eyes around me. I think they might attack or laugh at me, but there is absolutely no change. This is even more unnerving. I am being escorted to the unknown by creatures insistent upon my solitude. Even they refuse to interact with me. Fine. I can do this.

I have survived the storms. I have survived the darkness. I survived the scavenging and the shadows, and I have survived the journey no one else dared to take. I have survived this long waking to doorways leading into darkness, and the lightning that strikes right before loss. I have withstood starvation and I have managed to keep my wits about me even as I heard each of my companions die. I have no heroes except the hero within myself. I think I can survive a group of cowardly, silent torturers. They do not know the depth of my spirit.

From the vast abyss that is my strength right now, I pull up the memory of a story that Friend once told me. He was always a wellspring of stories and songs. Sometimes he joked that he was a bard, the most useless of people in a place like this. But I always admired him for his choice to become a Folklorist.

"We are lucky to have a bard in our midst," I told him once and he laughed at me, raising his eyebrows at the title I have given him.

"Why's that, Little Owl?"

"Because, someday we are going to go back to the surface and find that we have forgotten to preserve libraries. When that happens, people are going to be extremely grateful for those who have studied stories and histories and culture."

I know now that, even if we never get back to the surface and even if we never have enough people to re-establish society, I will always be grateful for the stories Friend has shared with me.

There were once two lovers, a musician who was the son of the goddess of music and could enchant any living soul with just one note that came from his lips or was plucked at his fingertips, and a very ordinary woman who is only remembered because of their love. If she had been someone special of her own accord, she would have her own story and never would have made it into his. As it is, even the most ordinary of women have a chance to be included in legends.

As is the case with so many legendary lovers, these two had a very short-lived romance. Shortly after their marriage, the woman was bitten by a snake, and died as the poison filled her veins. The musician could do nothing except what he had always done, which was play and sing.

Because grief filled his heart so completely, he could only sing in mourning and it made the whole world sad. All the birds stopped singing and flying, they fell from the sky the moment they heard him. All the flowers closed up and hid their faces. And the man wandered, searching for the half of him that he could not find.

Presently, the musician found himself at the temple of the gods. There was weeping intertwined with his singing, which upset the gods greatly, so they came down from Heaven to comfort him. They offered him wine and gold and the prettiest of their

*daughters to take the place of the wife he had lost,
and he sang all the louder to drown out their voices.*

*Not knowing what else to do, they took him
to the underworld and brought him before the king
and queen of the underworld, whereupon, the
musician fell silent. All of the gods and goddesses of
heaven and earth pleaded with the god of the
underworld to release the musician's wife and let
her return to the earth. Yet none of the gods could
sway nature's course.*

*So the musician picked up his guitar and
struck a chord that moved like a knife to cut deep
into the heart of each god. The queen of the
underworld began to cry as the musician sang out,
rattling the bones and bringing the gods to their
knees. He sang for the love in his heart that was
worth all the loss in the world, and he ended the
song with her name.*

*The king of the underworld was brought low
by the way the musician cried out her name and
knew that, even in the afterlife, she could hear him
and cried to return to him. So he released her and
they ran to embrace each other at the shores of the
underworld.*

*"Please." Said the musician, "Let her come
home with me!"*

*The king of the underworld agreed, yet no
task against nature is without challenge. To bring*

his wife back to life, the musician was instructed to walk in front of her and neither of them was to look back as they walked through the labyrinth of the undead. If these instructions were not carried out exactly, his wife would be carried away by the undead and never seen again.

This was just fine by the musician's wife, who had seen enough of the underworld. She walked behind her husband and never looked around once. Her husband, however, had never walked those lands before and fear seized him. He wondered if this was all just a dream and he had no way of knowing if his precious wife was actually there or if some terrible demons had taken her.

Finally, he could not take the fear anymore and, when the next doubt entered his mind, he instinctively looked back to make sure his wife was there. As soon as he did, he watched a demon snatch her away from him forever. Her scream echoed in his ears and heart and ever after its echo found a way into every song he sang. He could not escape it, so he fell silent. He refused the call of his music until one day, when it grew too hard of a burden to bear. He died, spending eternity in the underworld searching for the demon in the labyrinth of the dead who stole his wife from him.

My recollection of the story is not the very same as the version Friend told me. He is a lot better storyteller than I am, but I try to remember what he told me about savoring the details and not rushing to the climax of the story, so I hope what I remember is close in spirit to his version.

I can picture him beside me, listening as I recite his story. A few unbidden tears creep into the corner of my eyes.

"Why are you crying, Little Owl?" He would say if he were here. I don't care if it is pitch black around us, he would have known. Somehow, he would have known.

"Why do such sad stories exist?" I ask aloud, just as I would ask in return were he here, swallowing the admission that I miss him.

"Yes, the story is sad, but I told it to you for a reason, didn't I? There is always a reason I tell you the stories I do. What is the reason for this story, Little Owl? What does it teach us?"

I don't like the answer. I don't say it, and if he were here, Friend would have scolded me with a little smile and would have stayed still, expectantly, until I admitted it.

"Don't look back."

"Yes, Little Owl, don't look back. Your loved ones are there, always, following you through the darkness, but you can't doubt it. You have to trust it. You have to let it be. You can't ever be

reassured by physical presence and you have to keep going. Little Owl, don't look back for us."

Nine

I keep at it. I alternate sleeping and eating when I feel weakest. Soon, the granola bars are nothing except wrappers which I've licked clean a few times each and keep in my backpack. The water runs out. I can't be making good time; I feel like I am taking mere steps between sleep-spans and I'm getting more and more frustrated with myself every time I need to stop and rest.

I wish I could see my surroundings- even just the tiniest peek- but it is useless to dwell on that thought. Actually, dwelling in general is a bad idea. I clear my mind and concentrate on my breathing, my steps. I note the feel of the ground below me and the rhythm of the length of my steps in comparison to where the tracks are.

They say that the best horseback riders can close their eyes and still be perfectly on-course, able to direct the horse with little more than a thought, because they are so in-tune with their equine counterparts. I try to do the same with these tunnels. I can navigate the earth, if I can know her well enough to predict where her dangers lie. In the midst of my pathetic attempt to become one with the tunnels, I run into a wall.

I have no idea that it is there, so when I hit it, I get knocked down hard. I take a moment to stare at it, even though I cannot see it any better than a moment ago. Why is there a wall? Has the tunnel collapsed? I stand to investigate.

It isn't a collapse. It is smooth, man-made. I run my hands over what feels to be concrete and notice that it isn't strictly a wall, it's an edge. Probably a platform edge. Well, I don't have much to lose. It takes a couple of tries for my quivering arms to pull me onto the platform, but I do.

Once up here, I have no idea what to do. I get on my knees, and start to crawl around, feeling for anything that might be there, exploring. If there is a way out of this hell-hole, it would be through a platform, wouldn't it? I mean, the platforms used to lead to stairwells, which led to stations, which led to stairwells, which led outside- to the surface. So I feel for something that might be a door. I guess.

I find a bench, barely missing knocking myself out on it. I'm doing really well on my dexterity today. I also find a garbage can and promptly, accidentally knock it over. I make a mental note of where the mess is, but I'm pretty sure the smell will alert me if I get too close to it.

I keep exploring and find something smooth in front of me. It is cold, like stone, but a queasy feeling tells me stones aren't normally left lying around on platforms. I swallow my nausea and keep feeling it, trying to figure out what it is. Some sort of film comes off on my fingers. I'm about ready to abandon it, when my thumb pushes through a soft spot. Now I'm really, really regretting touching this thing.

Something squishes. This is not good, but I've gone this far... Oh. A horrible, horrible smell envelops me! There are two more holes near the first and more film and something sticky. I've figured out what it is. I drop the skull and vomit all over it.

The bile stings my parched throat. Ugh, I don't even have any water left to wash out the taste. I spit as much as possible, but it's not quite enough. I back up, reach into my bag, and take out the granola bar wrappers, licking at them again. It doesn't help much. I throw them on the platform, which I have essentially, gloriously trashed. If anyone has to ever do this again it is going to be very unpleasant for them...

I crawl around the vomit-covered corpse and smack my pretty little head into a wall. Damn it! I put my hand on the wall and steady myself as the world spins a little bit. I do not want to throw up again. Please, little stomach, don't throw up again! I swallow and swallow again. Taking my cues from last time, I try to feel the top of the wall. I cannot while on my knees, so I stand. Still no top. Great. So now I get to shimmy around the wall and hope to high heaven that I do not step in anything.

I make sure I do two things before each step: one, I feel along the wall with my hand. Two, I kick at the ground with the toe of my boot. I'm starting to think maybe this was a waste of time and an overall bad decision. Then, my hand touches something smooth and round and either cold or damp. Because there's no way a skull can be this far off the ground, I decide to feel it more. It is small enough that it my fingers can wrap around it easily. It is, I decide, a doorknob.

Now, a doorknob isn't really something to celebrate, it doesn't automatically mean a good or productive thing; there are many doorways that lead to dead-ends and bad dreams. However, this is the first thing I've discovered on this platform that even has a chance of being helpful. I turn the doorknob and, to my actual surprise, the door opens.

At this precise moment, that little voice in my head that is supposed to warn me when I'm about to do something really stupid, that has been as quiet as a dead man since Friend was taken, decides to wake up and start yelling at me. Yeah, I am aware that this could be the worst thing I could ever do. I could be walking into my doom; the outcome is uncertain.

However, the outcome of going back is fixed. I will die if I go back, most likely covered in someone else's body fluids and my own vomit and, knowing the way things have been going, trash. I can't go any farther on licking wrappers and flipping off demons. So I go through the door and I shut it behind me.

I think about taking a step, but realize there could be anything in the world in here, so I let myself succumb to the kneeling thing again. It's a little degrading, this way of exploring. I wonder how Sights ever stayed sane. Or, for that matter, how he survived traveling without seeing, yet without crawling around like an insect of some kind.

Eventually, after getting turned around even more times than I care to admit, I find the stairwell. I crawl up the stairs, too. I wonder how close I am to ripping the knees of my wrap-pants. The fabric is sturdy, but I do not know how long I've been crawling or how much more of it I will have to do.

There is a platform after about thirty steps. Despite being a little more cheerful than before, I don't have enough energy to hold myself up on my arms anymore. I lay down, using my pack as a pillow as always. I lie on my side, with my arms underneath the pack-pillow in an effort to get them to stop shaking so violently. It's colder on the concrete than it was on dirt, so I curl into a little ball and, though it takes a bit longer, I do sleep.

I wake stiff and with a horrible taste in my mouth. A snippet of song catches in my mind. *Hello darkness, my old friend. You have come to me again.* I don't know any more of it, though, so I let it fall away with the memory of a dream I can't keep. I'm utterly exhausted, despite just having slept. I really hope the station is nearby, the next stairwell isn't as long, and the outside door isn't locked. If all of those hopes come through, my next hope is there is food and water outside.

I climb the stairs, trying to distract myself by thinking of all the stories and songs I know of that include stairs. Winnie the Pooh starts out with stairs. My mom read that aloud to me and my sister when we were kids and, forever after, we would drag our stuffed animals down the stairs by their feet, bending over a bit if we had to, to make sure they went *bump, bump, bump* like Pooh.

There's a good chunk of Lord of the Rings dedicated to stairs. Tolkien's stairs are probably more like mine than Pooh's are. This place is dark, I'm crawling steadily upwards, there's probably a terrifyingly giant spider that will jump out and attack me soon. Yeah, I'm living in a real Mordor entrance. Only, without any sort of guide or gardener and I do not plan on passing through this place again to go back. Also, and I suppose this is the biggest difference, the fate of the world really isn't relying on me.

Those are the only two stories I can think of with stairs in them. I'm tired of thinking and my brain is tired enough that it is just circling around the same thoughts. It is a bad sign, one that tells me I'm about to pass out. *Ok, so you've thought of stories.* I tell myself. *Now what about songs? What are some songs about stairs?* It is a long while before I think of the painfully obvious Stairway to Heaven. I don't even know that song, but it has stairs in it! I can't coax myself to get out of my mental spiral of exhaustion to think of any others, so I give up trying and focus on moving upwards one step at a time.

Finally, the stairs end. I must be in the station now. It will be bigger than the platform, and there will be some sort of gated window that once served as a ticket booth for the subway system. *I must try very hard not to run into that*, I remind myself.

Each movement I take begins with me stretching out one hand straight out into the air before me and waving my arm a bit, just to make sure that I do actually find the gate before hitting it. Because I do this, I am better at finding things. I find two more benches before I find the gate, which is locked. Just perfect.

I climb over the gate and fall over the other side. It takes a moment or two for me to get enough energy to go on. I want to just stay there and sleep more. It actually takes a great deal of will power to not just stay there and sleep until I die, but the will power is there if I dig deep enough. I roll over, tearing at my throat with a groan. *Keep crawling, songbird, owl, bird thing. Find your way to the stairs.*

I don't know how, but I find the stairs and I manage to drag myself up them. Midway up the stairs, is a landing. Mercifully, there is a garbage can, and I rummage through it like a child would rummage through a toy box. I find the treasure of the day near the bottom of the bin, a half-empty bottle of liquid. Suppressing the simultaneous urges to chug it and throw it away because I cannot see what the liquid is or what is in the liquid... I take a sip before I can think better of it.

It is, thankfully, water. Old, stale water that tastes like plastic, but still water and there are a lot worse things the water could taste like. I sip it slowly, like my mother taught me, and make sure I drink it all before heading on. I do not scavenge food from the trash. I learned long ago that that is a good way to get sick, and I cannot afford to be sick right now, even if it is just food poisoning. It would mean losing this last little bit of water. Keeping water in my stomach must be put before the desire for food. I am happy that I am cognizant enough to rationalize this even as my stomach growls its displeasure at me.

I realize that I've been clenching my jaw. I drop it a little, making sure I stop grinding my teeth. My mother used to tell me that grinding teeth would give me headaches. I do not need anything else to weigh me down and motivate me to just give up. *Light as air*, I tell myself, *I'm light as air. I'm a songbird, an owl, and I will yet fly.*

I come to the top of the stairs where the world comes to an abrupt end. The stairwell is blocked off by something large and heavy that feels of wood and dust. I throw my weight upward, but it doesn't budge. Suddenly, claustrophobia hits with what could be the most devastating stab of reality ever thrust upon me. Now what?

I grunt a list of profanities at the impassible partition as I run my fingers over it, searching for a door knob or some way to open it. I do so with caution, however, because the wood is uneven and old, and I do not want to get slivers. It creaks a little when I touch it. I imagine it would recoil if it could.

Suddenly, a chunk breaks off and falls upon me. I throw my arms over my head and most of the big chunks hit them. I still wind up with splinters in my hair, but no major injuries, so I am thankful for that. I reach through what is left of the wooden plank and find something plastic on the other side. This moves the tiniest bit when I push on it. Not enough to actually get through it, but at least it is something.

Part of the problem is that I can't reach it very well. The middle is a good four or five steps down the stairs and I do not have the right leverage to be able to push it open from there. From where I can actually reach the plastic well, there's very little give. I wonder if it is nailed down, as so many covers were when the stairway entrance was not in an actual building.

I go back to the landing where I found the water and empty the trash can. It takes much more effort than I can afford to drag its metal frame up the stairs and lift it up over my head to push against the plastic. A fantastically overpowering and horrid stench washes over me as I hold onto the opening and push the bottom upward. Something sticky drips on my shoulder.

I put all my effort into it. I conserve none of it for afterward. If there is to be an afterward, it will have to come with nourishment of its own.

However, if I don't get this plastic off, I will be stuck in this hellish pit forever. Sweat drips into my left eye, stinging it. I try my best to ignore it and, with one last desperate curse of damnation into the night, the plastic comes free and I sprawl forward, plummeting down the stairs.

Fortunately I catch myself at the landing and emerge only shaken and bruised and with stubborn, unwelcome tears on my cheeks, rolling under my nose. I let the trash bin roll the rest of the way, following the clashing of it as if I could see the trail of sound bouncing to the station floor.

I look into the shadow-consumed station and the nothingness it offers, a petty compensation for all it has taken for price. I see the foreboding luminescent twin green lights in the station. Calm and lingering, they wait for something that I cannot imagine is very pleasant. I turn away and climb back up, gasping like a drowned sailor trying to find her way to the surface. My heart pounds in my ears. Time is running out, and I need air.

I cannot imagine that this will work, but I have to try. Since the part of the plastic that has come loose is too far off the ground for me to reach, I lie down on the top step, propping myself up on my elbows, and push against the rotting wood and heavy plastic with my shoulder and head. I scooch along the edge of the now-boarded entry, half of me gripping the wall with all my might, the other half dangling helplessly down, waiting to fall.

Down below me the Thunderbourne watch with absent eyes. I waver and spend a moment kicking at the wall with my dangling leg, willing my grandfather's boots to find a steady grip. They do, eventually. I'm pretty sure now that I am going to die here.

No. I can at least die in the sun. I'm almost there, and I owe it to those who wander and die in darkness to lead their souls to light. If I can find even a sliver of light to penetrate this hell, it will be enough. Once I get out, I can die. But not yet. Not yet.

I can smell the wind. After the weight of damp, dark air, I start to laugh at the foolish hope of it all. I may yet get out! I slide a hand out, slowly, under the loose plastic, then an arm, a shoulder, and my head. And it is like this, half-in, half-out that I take a first look at my new freedom.

My heart sinks at the sight. There is nothing. No sign of civilization, no plant life or creature or bird. Not even a drop of sunlight. Everything is bare and empty: dead grass and patches of soggy swampland and remnants of pavement. The sky is overcast and gray, dark enough that my eyes only slightly burn in adjustment to the shade. This is hardly worth anything. There is just as much death here as below. But there is wind here; gentle and soothing and cool. It is so unlike the whipping, screaming wind I remember from before, the wind I fear and, in dreams, relive.

I pull myself out and stand up straight. This is the world. Now what?

Ten

I spend fourteen wake-spans wandering around the barren remains of this skeleton city. The cloud cover makes it impossible to tell the passing of time. I know that somewhere, the sun is still in the sky, but it has not showed its face unveiled by clouds since I've surfaced. The sky is just one more unending horizon of gray. I'm amazed that time, which once dictated every single living organism on this planet, could be so fragile. Time has been felled and maybe I will be the last one to remember it.

My wake-spans are shorter now, my sleep-spans longer, to make up for the lack of nutrients. Bodies get energy from light, food, water, and sleep. Since I only have access to one of those on a regular basis, I abuse the privilege. I kept the water bottle from my last moments underground, so I use that to collect rainwater and, when rain doesn't come, water from the marshes. The roots of the grasses, although dead and taste like dirt, are edible enough to sustain me.

I survey the layout of the city I call Skeleton. I walk the middle of the old, broken roads and touch the foundations of what would have been a house. There are three parks, all of which now form the marshes. There is also a city pool which is now, still, a pool, although filled with grime and film. I can only guess that it was not drained before all of this happened. I do not touch the grime in the pool.

I make a game out of what I think the city used to look like, what buildings stood where and how tall they could have been. When I am bored, I make them so tall that even the many birds, which I always put in my make-believe Skeleton, cannot fly high enough to see the sun reflect off the top floor offices. I make up little families that work there, and walk them home when I imagine the sun goes down so they can sleep.

I do not sleep in any of the Skeleton houses; it is too sad to do so. Instead, I've made up a small shelter in a corner of what was probably downtown Skeleton where I discovered a collapsed concrete parking garage. There is a special little entry into the structure, which leads to a beautiful sight of concrete and tiny flower-like weeds, the only plants to be sheltered from the harsh weather.

I never pick the little white things that grow in creeping vines, but I lean over and smell them and they hug themselves to my nose, like they've waited an eternity to be discovered and do not want me to ever leave. Sometimes I do not leave them.

Sometimes I spend all day in my little house, singing to them and telling them the stories I've gathered along the way here. It's less lonely talking with the weeds I call flowers than the ghosts I call people.

It is warmer with the flowers, as well. The cool breeze leaves my cheeks flushed and raw. On a particularly cold day, I go back to the tunnel entrance and rip off the plastic and the remainder of the wood and line the portion of my house where I sleep with it. The wood is warmer than concrete against my back and the plastic keeps out the rain. I always keep my backpack under shelter because that's all I have in the world, and I aim to keep it as long as the world aims to keep me.

There are some spans of vast loneliness. The spirits who followed me through the tunnel wander around here, popping up to remind me of my loss in the most random of times and places. They seem empty, like footprints more than actual people. I realize it is like a bizarre phantom-limb syndrome only, instead of limbs, they are presences of people. The phantoms of my underground path are both my poison and solace in this place.

Mostly, though, it is quiet. I forget the difference between thinking and speaking. I dance in silence, pray in the corners of Skeleton which seem most sacred, and I never once think about the future beyond this one city. That is, until I stumble upon a hilltop at the edge of Skeleton and am reminded of the magnitude of the Earth.

The vastness of the horizon creates a vague agoraphobia in the core of my heart where something turns and stabs and yearns at the damaged beauty before me. I cannot move for a long time. I linger in limbo. Time passes in weather: it mists and rains and the wind strengthens at my back. Then, from behind me, a cold chill unrelated to the weather spreads down my spine.

I turn around and there is a tall shadow of a stranger peering down at me through spiritless jade eyes. It is a formless figure that hovers menacingly, yet peacefully, before me: a void of every aspect of life in the very essence- or absence of essence- this creature possesses. It is as if some hole were cut in the fabric of reality from the space in which this creature exists. It moves and eats every color, every smell, every thought, every emotion, consuming even the fear of it being before me until all that exists between it and me is the painful pounding of my heart and the consciousness of how much *more* the Thunderbourne is than me.

I am intrigued and frightened beyond my own understanding, wondering how many lives this creature has followed, dissected, devoured, and rejected. How many times has it looked for something that cannot fill its own void? It acts curious, yet I know it already knows the outcome of every attack, which makes me wonder why the Thunderbourne kill at all. There can be no passion behind the attacks, no pleasure, no fulfillment of curiosity, no vengeance; this creature is pure *nothing* and, therefore, there can be no reason for any of their behavior. And all of this I can see in its eyes, because nothing is in its eyes.

It doesn't even acknowledge me. It might as well be looking, as I was, at the vast scenery of the forgotten surface world. Yet, somehow the vacancy burrows into me. I find myself on my knees before the Thunderbourne, begging for it to stop. But it can't, because it is not doing anything.

It holds me captive for as long as it wants, then releases me and fades away, like a wave backing away into the ocean. I let go of the fistfuls of dead grass I've torn away from the earth and the breath I've been holding for forever. I stand and walk through the city once more and see the emptiness within it, the complete and utter pointlessness of being here alone.

For the first time, the pavement and foundations of Skeleton, overrun with dead grass and wind, really resemble a Skeleton. The city is gone. The weeds are quiet. The souls have disappeared. And the Thunderbourne follows me, unseen, as I pick up my bag, sling it over my shoulder, and find a new path and a new determination: to find someone to fill the void in my spirit.

The journey through the Surface is not very much different than the way through the Underground and, yet, it is fundamentally opposite. It is more than the airflow and space; it is the complete lack of evidence of the human race. The Underground violated every sense with a reminder that humans exist, even in the rare clumps of shivering fear. Even the existence of the Underground is proof of human hands realized in the smell of human filth and the uncanny way darkness makes one feel like there is always something or someone invadingly close.

Here, even with the corpses of cities, it feels like the earth herself birthed a dead society. Humans did not create this world, nature did. And nature, in turn, destroyed it and claims it again. Within the first moments of seeing this world, I would be willing to bet my life that there is not a single human that ever walked here or ever will walk again. There isn't even the potential for humans to rehabilitate the earth. There is nothing from or for us here.

Walking through the deliberate exile of mankind is unsettling. Yet, I feel honored that I could be chosen to be the one human let back onto the surface. I remember to honor whatever force drove us out, treating everything with care. The fistfuls of grass are the first and last of the Earth's resources that I have destroyed without specific survival reason since I emerged here.

For that reason, I specifically avoid every single road I come across. When I find one, I go over it or turn and leave it behind. I want nothing to do with the humans whom the earth seems to think deserved their fate. As foolish as it sounds, I want to stay on the good side of whoever runs this world now, if anyone. I want to be allowed to stay here, and I have no urge to fix any of this.

When the wind blows a certain way, the world is frigid. I curl up into a little ball when I sleep. I cover my face with my scarf, and wish I had brought that piece of plastic to ward away the wind, although I know I would never be able to drag it anywhere. Realistically, shelter is not feasible, but my mind refuses to grasp that concept. It still wants and whines for warmth during slumber.

As is, the sleep-spans are terrible. I never fall completely asleep and I never truly wake, and the deprivation makes things colder and more miserable. I start to think maybe I was wrong to have left my flower-friends back at Skeleton. Of course, the doubt always comes when the goings are tough. I wasn't wrong to leave; there was nothing for me back there. The only choice is to keep going.

I go until the pavement fades away into a sea of swampland that swallows dead, gray trees and tall, willowy grasses. The ground sponges beneath me. Pretty soon the marshes will be above my boots. I look around at the swamp that stretches as far as my eyes can see and my brain can imagine. I cannot go through the water. Even if I could stand the cold, and even if the water levels didn't go high enough that I would have to swim, where would I sleep? What would I eat? Can I drink this water?

I keep the swamp always in sight on my right hand side and search for a way around it. When I feel the earth start to slide away, I sidestep until it solidifies. It is strange, feeling the crackling grass snap underfoot one step and slipping on swamp the next. When I wander too far away, so that I stop squishing into swamp, I turn and walk towards the marshes until I find the moisture again. This ensures that I follow the curvature of the swamp, instead of loosing it.

Consequently, I follow the edge of the swamp until I do not remember what direction I was initially going. Now there is just forwards and backwards. Between the two, I will always choose forwards if I can help it. Isn't that what this is all about? Going forward when everything stops, when everything in life is against you, you go forward anyway.

I imagine what it would have been like to take the first steps on this soil. Mindful of the feel of the grass underfoot and the way the wind smells, I pretend, for a moment, that I am a great adventurer trying to find the perfect spot to civilize. Of course, not this patch, it is too exposed to the elements. Not that patch either, it is too wet, but the ancient explorers must not have known where they were going or what they would find, and that is some comfort to me now.

I wonder what the earth looked like so long ago, before human hands built everything new. Did it look like it looks now, after it all? I heard once that most of the world was forested in the old days. It is hard to imagine the world covered in trees, or covered in anything really. I barely even remember how it was covered in buildings and filled with people.

Most of the trees were gone by the time we moved into the city, cut down for urban expansion and technological advancement. When I was very small, we lived in a run-down farmhouse and there was a patch of trees on our neighbor's property, which my sister and I deemed a forest. We had never seen so many trees in one place, although there probably really had been only ten or fifteen trees. Jenna and I played there almost every afternoon never knowing we were innocently trespassing.

I don't remember the games we played, only flashes of running and chasing and climbing until our palms were so sticky with sap that it took days to be able to hold anything paper or cloth without residue. There was a particular tree that we used to climb. It was our secret place, my sister's and mine, where we would go to watch the world pass by and scribble in notebooks, pretending we were writing.

Before we moved into the city, Jenna and I collected a piece of bark and some leaves from our tree and put them in a small keepsake box. Our notebooks, which were filled with secret words that meant everything to us and nothing to anyone else, were also placed into the treasure box. We buried the box in the yard of our city home and we- I- did not think to go back for it when the storms came.

There were so many things we lost in the storms. Every childhood plaything and cherished keepsake was scattered in the wind. I know that survival is key, that when we fled we did so because life is more precious than material possessions. Still, when you are a child, there are some things in your toy box that are like life to you. Dolls, stuffed animals, pictures I drew, a blanket from my cradle, baby clothes, my sister's teddy bear that she kept with her always, my father's Sunday records, are all irreplaceably a part of me that is gone.

When I was little, I wanted to be an adventurer. I dreamed and pretended all the time that I was someone who set out throughout the world with only the clothes on my back and the knowledge of which plants were good to eat on a quest to save the human race. Now, here I am, living out that naive wish, wishing I could go back to a time when I was just an ordinary, one-in-a-million girl.

I come to a part of the marshes that looks more like a lake than anything and, since the wind has slowed a bit, I decide to take the time to wash myself. I, of course, did not have the luxury of bathing or washing very often in the Underground. No one did. It was one of the sources of the stench. Since I have surfaced, however, I have deliberately taken the time to wash as often as I can find clean-looking water.

This is one of those times, so I remove my boots and socks. Sitting at the water's edge, I soak my socks, balling them up and scrubbing them against themselves to remove as much of the dirt as I can. Then I lay them out on the shore, and begin to strip away the rest of my clothing. Because I have two layers of almost everything, I've been alternating which layer I wash at a time so I'm never caught wearing cold, wet clothes unless it rains.

This time, I wash my underwear, wrap-pants, and tank top. I wear my leggings and bra as I wash my face, neck, chest, and underarms by cupping water and splashing it onto those areas. I also roll up my leggings and wash my feet. Then I lean my head very close to the water and wash what little hair I have.

Due to irregular patterns of maintenance, most people in my camp cut off all their hair when they went Underground. It is just easier that way, and more comfortable. My hair cannot be more than a few inches long and most of that length came while I was traveling, because I did not trim it myself and would never have asked our company to trim it for me.

I dry off using Hugs' scarf, then wash it too. I slip on my jacket and the pair of socks I used to make my grandfather's boots fit better. I tie my wrap-pants and scarf to my backpack, stuff the tips of the socks and underwear into the elastic waist of my leggings, and loop the arm holes of my tank top through my belt before moving on. That way the wind will dry them, but I will not have to wait before continuing my journey.

It actually feels nice to shed some of my clothing. I imagine I look like some bad-ass character from a virtual reality game and indulge myself by strutting a few steps like the overly-sexualized characters would, were they in my place. It is ridiculous, actually, because no one who survives this long would ever, in a million years, resemble the idealized men and women of those games.

Although I was not always, I am pretty thin now, mostly from lack of proper nutrition and the almost-constant movement. However, with the weight, I also lost a great deal of healthy-looking complexion, the majority of my too-small-to-start-with breasts, and, of course, some hygiene. I would not consider this version of me sexy in the slightest, especially with a load of laundry strapped to me.

When my clothes are dry, I put them back on. I'm tired enough that I will wait to do the other layer until I've slept. I do not want to have to worry about wet clothes when I sleep. I wander a little further, until the wind has all but died out and a hazy warmth settles over the land. This is the perfect time to rest. For once I might not wake up to a shivering that I cannot shake off.

Eleven

I sleep surprisingly well, although it starts to sprinkle warm droplets as I drift back into consciousness. I'm not too concerned as the temperature is pleasant and the rain light. I adjust my pack so that it sits underneath my jacket just in case the mist turns into a shower, which it does, and walk on.

Soon my road takes an incline upwards, over a hill. The marshes fall away from the hill and I let it go, staying true to the course I have set. I am thankful that my grandfather's boots have decent traction. The rain loosens the earth and causes a few mini mudslides down the hill. I slip a couple of times, but nothing major, and manage to the top with only undoing the washing on my wrap-pants, which are now splashed with mud.

I am utterly unprepared for the sight that lies out before me beyond the hill. Miles and miles of stuff floods the valley, trash and treasure as if every proof of human existence had been pushed and gathered here to rot. It looks like a giant junkyard. Anything that was not completely destroyed by the storms was blown here. I see houses, whole houses, and cars, and everything piled on top of each other in a great and terrible, chaotic, masterpiece of human-made belongings.

I am thrown off balance by a gust of wind and stumble forward, down the hill. I take a few uneasy steps, slide a couple inches, and then regain composure. I go to the edge of the human things and take it all in. From down here I can see just how much more broken everything is. There is a thin layer of broken glass over most everything, and pieces of walls and roofs seem to have everything pinned down.

I search for something to pick up. Everything around this edge is trash, so I choose to pick up an old CD. The label is worn off, so I do not know what this piece of musical history holds. I turn it over. Through a rainbow, half-scratched out reflective surface, I catch sight of my unevenly trimmed hair, a shade or two darker than the dead, golden grass. My gray, distant eyes look wild and haunted. I'm lost in my own story as I stare at myself for the first time since the storms. When did I grow up?

I don't exactly look like someone different than the picture presented to me by the last mirror I confronted, but different enough to frighten me. I am changed enough that I no longer know me. I see a sad woman with eyes perpetually as open as they can go to see through darkness as vast as the destruction it conceals. I can envision how my face morphed through age and hunger and loss like a video clip set on repeat, from the nineteen year old girl that fled the sun to now, the woman whom souls follow into the unknown; the woman strong enough to survive, yet not strong enough to save.

I wonder how many years have actually passed since the day we fled. We could see the purple clouds rolling in behind us. My grandfather grabbed his supplies, and I grabbed my father's camera and we met my mom at the shelter where she worked. The whole building began to shake while we were still inside and all the lights flickered off. All of us dropped to our knees and covered our heads as the wailing wind whipped through our town, shattering windows and rolling cars and killing everyone who had stayed home instead of evacuating to the shelter as ordered by the city.

We spent days in the shelter and not a single hour passed by when we could not hear the scream of the storm. The lights never came back; we made do with the flashes of lighting that touched down every couple of seconds so quickly that the thunder could not keep up with it. It was like the world's longest running and deadliest fireworks display. There was hail, for a while, yet surprisingly little rain. When the wave was over, there was not enough of our town to justify staying, even half of our shelter was gone, and so we left. We survived.

Only, apparently, I did not really survive. I died and was reborn as someone else. I am a survivor, who once was Songbird, who once was Little Owl, who once was someone else entirely. I am the one who fades away every step of the way, yet who asks in vain for everyone else to remain. From now one, I will be Fade, and my name will remind me that I am not the same as I was before, each wake-span I begin again, and neither does anyone else remain. We are not who we are when we fall asleep. We are who we are when we rise and walk and survive.

I drop the CD. My vision is too blurry to see myself anyway. I clear my eyes with my wrist and look at the remains before me, choosing to see past the corpse of my beloved world, choosing instead to see a place where I can do what I need to. I prioritize my thoughts and push aside everything that will not help me be the survivor I need to be.

First of all, I need to find supplies. Friend, a wellspring of useful knowledge, taught me to scavenge. Now is my chance to prove myself to his teaching. I tie the scarf to my face, to block out any small particles of glass or dust or whatever else might be here, and dig into the junkyard.

At first there is only wood and shingles and siding but, as I get farther into the hoard of destroyed belongings, I start to find semblances of treasures. There is a little girl's jewelry box, with a twirling ballerina inside. The key is missing to make the music play and the ballerina dance, but there are a few safety pins inside, which I take. I used to have a music box just like this when I was small. I set it carefully aside, not willing to drop it and risk it breaking, not willing to touch it any longer.

I lift a shattered pile of dresser and accidentally tip over a cracked, plastic cooler. The contents, about half a dozen cans of vegetables and an opened box of cereal, spill out. I gather the canned goods, even the peas, which I hate, and put them in my bag. The cans almost fill up the bag, but not quite, so I continue my search.

I really need to find water, but necessity does not dictate outcome, and I have no luck locating any. I stop and allow myself to eat a can of food. I'm very, very hungry. However, as I re-examine the plentiful stores that I have just gathered, I realize that I am not hungry enough, or desperate enough, to eat the peas. So I open a can of creamed corn, instead, hoping that the cream will somewhat make up for lack of water.

When I start my scavenging again, I try a new spot. Again, on the surface, everything is broken homes and shattered glass, and dust. I move what probably once was an antique writing desk. I do not know that it is such a treasure until I move it. Unmoved, its back is facing me and the back of furniture never reveals how beautiful it is. When I heave it over, I see the beautiful carved wood retain its shape for only a moment before it crashes apart. My stomach churns at the lost beauty. *It doesn't matter anymore*, I try to tell myself. *Everything beautiful and everything ugly is all destroyed now.*

I look back to see what was under the gorgeous desk and my churning stomach lurches. There are dozens of skeletons strewn across the ground. Most of them are animal remains; dogs or cats or squirrels, one or two birds, but there are also humans in the mix. Every body is deformed in some way; broken bones or a spine that curves in the wrong direction, and all of the humans jaws are wide open like they died screaming.

I back away. If ever this leg of the journey was a childhood adventure or an honor bestowed on me to see the earth again, it stops being so right now. The hairs on the back of my neck bristle and I draw my knife. There is probably nothing out here anymore, but even the most remote possibility makes me obsessed with defending myself against it.

I spin around, searching for the cause, some physical reason for all of this. I find myself looking up at the hill. It has stopped raining, but the moisture in the air still clings closely to the earth. There is the unmistakable form of a tall human at the top of the hill, all form and shadow and unwavering eyes and not at all human in any way beyond outline.

I want to yell out a challenge at the Thunderbourne. Instead, I glare back at the creature, filling my eyes with all the emotion the Thunderbourne will never express. I stand over the bodies of the dead, knife ready to wield in a combat I know will never take place. The demon stares at me from the hilltop, then raises two shadow-arms out from its body, the formlessness dripping off the arms like massive wings. It catches the wind and soars down the hill towards me, stopping right in front of me.

It is so tall, so menacing, before me. Behind it, the sky darkens into a threatening deep purple. The wind picks up, and I drop my grandfather's knife. The Thunderbourne moves its left wing, which now holds the outline of a human arm and hand again, with alarming speed until the palm of its nothingness hand hovers over the knife, just inches away from touching my right shoulder.

The knife stops mid-air, and hovers back into my hand. The Thunderbourne closes its fist and I close my fist around the knife and sheathe it. The creature reaches to me like it is about to touch my face and pierces my eyes with its own. Somewhere, far beneath the nothing, I see hunger. For an unblinking second, I wonder what it feels like to die.

There are creatures of Friend's stories, of mythology, who are immortal and hate it. They seek out mortal humans and torture them to death because they envy the ability to die. They are fascinated by how the human body responds to death and every moment of dying is beautiful to them. Is that what this creature is? Are the Thunderbourne obsessed with death? Are they immortal?

Right before the hand of nothing, quivering ever so slightly, touches me, it drops back to the side of the Thunderbourne. The demon draws itself up, making itself taller than ever before, and takes its eyes off me. It looks over my left shoulder at some far away thing. Slowly, I look as well. My heart leaps up into my throat, forcing a small cry into the air. Across the way, is another human being.

Twelve

I think it is a magician. The other human being, wearing a long, colorful coat, spins and jumps around upon the junk pile as if it were jumping over a creek on stones. I have to look twice to make sure I'm not watching a butterfly. I can't take my eyes off the blatant display of blue and yellow and orange grace fluttering around above the last remains of humanity. It's as mesmerizing as the Thunderbourne's eyes, only I'm watching everything instead of staring down nothing.

I quickly glance back. The Thunderbourne is gone. Not knowing how to deal with everything that has just happened, I slip quietly down, sitting with my knees pulled up to my chest behind the cover of an expensive-looking car. I try to process everything; feeling the Thunderbourne's need to destroy me, then turning around and finding something in existence that I never thought to see ever again. I can't do it. I can't go back. I'm literally sitting between death and beauty and I want nothing to do with either. But I cannot just walk away from what could be the only human being left in the world beside me. Don't I owe it to somebody to speak with this person?

On the other hand, there is no one else on earth to owe except myself and whoever this *person* is? If anything, I owe it to myself to walk away. Nothing good can come from this. I do not know anything about the man or woman in the magician's coat. They could be a serial killer. Hell, they could be responsible for the skeletons on the ground. They could be the reason why the Thunderbourne gave me back my knife.

Only, that would imply that the Thunderbourne was a friend and a protector. I'm not ready to address that. I can't process the implications that would come along with the idea that the Thunderbourne is an angel, not a demon. I don't understand how everything in my life turns itself around on top of each other. The demon is a friend and the human is a killer dancing over the corpses of its victims? What twisted joke is this life?

I grip my grandfather's knife with both hands, breathing in controlled exhales meant to steady my racing heart. I turn my head toward where I know the person is, although I am too well covered to actually see them. I do not owe it to anyone to give this person a chance, but I do owe it to myself to know who the enemy is here. I turn myself around, so that I am crouching on one knee behind the thrown-open door of the convertible with ruined seats. I switch the knife to my right hand, blade faced downward, and make my way as quietly as I can through the rubble. I am hunting a human.

Soon, I am close enough that I can hear the other human singing to themselves. It isn't a tune I recognize, and the words are in another language. The voice is a clear tenor, so I think it is a man that I am stalking. I allow myself a quick glance to place myself. It is a man, slightly younger than myself, with dark curls bouncing around at his shoulders as he moves in some self-choreographed half-dance, half-martial arts sequence.

He leaps toward the edge of the junk pile and shrugs off his coat, which, I see now, is entirely patchwork, and throws it to the grass. From the pockets of ripped-apart jeans he produces two butterfly knives and proceeds to put on a wonderful display of skill for no one except himself and the skeletons he may or may not have created. Damn. He's brilliant.

I stop. There is no way I can take this man on if it came to confrontation. I fall back against something broken- I can't recognize what it was- and let my head bang against it perhaps a little too hard. I freeze, certain he heard me, but when he doesn't show up to slaughter me, I relax. I close my eyes and open them. I look around and rest my head against the white-washed wood thing again. I sigh, than calm my breathing again.

I need to figure out what to do. I cannot compete with his skill in weaponry. If I am to have the upper hand when- if- I confront him, I need to get those knives away from him. Even so, if he's half as skilled at fist-fighting as he is wielding blades, I'm dead. What am I talking about? I've been a walking corpse since I let Sights pull me onto that platform. Might as well push my luck to the limits, right? And if all else fails, I could always run away. Running has worked so well for me so far.

I freeze. He's stopped singing. I hear the fall of his feet on a metal sheet right above me. I swear to myself in a moment of panic. Ever so carefully, with as little movement as possible, I look to my right. He is standing on a car door that is balanced on some shrapnel not three feet away. Thankfully, I'm still under cover, but very barely.

His knives remain in his smooth hands, but are at rest. He is looking down at something just beyond us through soft, intelligent brown eyes. He blinks and, not removing his gaze from the sight that has him hypnotized, puts one of the rainbow butterfly knives in his back right pocket and clutches a closed fist over an insignia I do not recognize on his long-sleeved thermal shirt. He bows his head and closes his eyes and it hits me, he's seen the skeletons.

The honor he shows them floors me. He can't have been the killer, not with a reaction like that. He seems genuinely shaken and sad by their presence. He opens his eyes and they are hard as he scans the horizon for I'm not sure what. However, because his attention is now focused on any possible movement, and I'm so close, I'm stuck. Just because he wasn't responsible for the deaths of the skeletons I uncovered, doesn't mean he wouldn't attack me impulsively, or consciously, if he discovered that I had been spying on him.

He makes one more visual sweep of the junkyard and lingers a little longer than I'd hoped on what was the writing desk. Then he turns and, as light-footed as ever, bounds away. I stay where I am, knowing better than to pop up until I am absolutely sure he is not looking back. I debate whether or not I want to follow him.

There is nothing to be gained following him. Except, perhaps, sating my curiosity about his survival. There is something about him that seems like light to me, something about his presence that I felt when he was nearby. It was warm and glowing, like he held the sun inside him, like he was hope incarnate. It seems silly to think of him that way, I don't know him, and he's just a human being, but what does that matter? I am just a human being, and I have survived. There is light inside of me, why can't it be inside him as well?

Ok, I'll follow him, if I can find a way to do so without giving away my position. However, I do not follow him to please my own heart or to let him find a way to help me; I do so to prove to myself that he is not anything special. We have survived by chance, both of us. We have that in common, but that is all. I do not need him in my life; I can survive alone. I was *meant* to survive alone. His being here is a coincidence, one I intend to prove to myself and move on.

I need to figure this out. How do I follow him without being seen? I take a glance over my left shoulder. He is digging through some of the rubble, scavenging, no doubt. I slide out of my coat and backpack. I use the pins I salvaged from the jewelry box to fix the broken strap on my backpack. I replace the coat and pack and recheck the status of the man.

He has produced a bag filled with something out of nowhere and is reclaiming his own coat. Maybe we have more in common than I thought. I push the thought away and move through the junk as best as I can, trying to avoid getting a palm filled with broken glass or rusty nails. I'm not as quiet as I would like to be, but if the man hears me, he does not act like it.

Once his coat is replaced, buttoned with silver, half-falling-off buttons, the man takes one more look towards where the skeletons lie in eternal agony. I flatten myself against the ground. If he takes the hill and journeys across the dead land, there's no way I can follow without being seen. I will have to confront him or let him go. If he continues through the miles of ruin, I will have cover, but it will be harder to track him. He looks between the moors and the ruin, as if he is choosing between the two. *The ruins. Please, pick the ruins.*

He, surprisingly, takes my mental suggestion and disappears into the junkyard. Ok, so he's fast as well as graceful and skillfully competent in the use of his knives. Add that to the list of things that make us different. I make my way to the edge of the grass and follow it until I come to the place where the man entered the junkyard. To my surprise, there is a pathway through the ruins. It is no wider than a deer trail, but it is enough. I follow it in pursuit of the man who should not exist.

The junk, piling up to his shoulders on both sides, does not seem to concern the man. He follows the trail in good spirit. Since I am almost always crouched as I follow after, the junk rises over my head. I dodge between broken headboards and overturned benches and pieces of structures, hiding when he turns to look back, taking chances when he is focused ahead.

When I was little, on hot summer days, my sister and I would walk barefoot on the street. To avoid burning our toes as we skittered from one place to the other, we would play a game. We pretended that the shady spots on the pavement, created by trees, were safe zones while the rest of the blacktop was enemy territory. We coined the phrase "quick through the sun, slow in the shade," and for years afterward, walking in the shade was always leisurely and walking through the radiance of the sun was always brisk. Moving from cover to cover now is like playing that game again. Except there is no sister by my side, and the threat of being seen is real.

It isn't long before the man picks up singing again, and I become an unknown audience to a full repertoire of songs that I have never heard before, but suit his voice perfectly. Most of the songs involve loving, and losing, a woman of considerable beauty and nobility. I wonder what the world would be like if there were as many songs about the broken hearts that beautiful men leave behind as there are about the futility of loving a woman.

Would our places be reversed, were that the case? Would I be the beautiful and talented magician while he, the lone survivor depending on luck and self-control secretly chased after me? After everything I've been through, I'm glad it is me walking here and him walking there. I wouldn't trade places with anyone for any sort of payment, even relief from my own emotional trauma. I could never wish my pain on another. It is far better that I carry my burdens that I have been conditioned to bear. Let any others who may still exist live freely; I am strong enough to play scapegoat this time around.

He has now cycled completely through his songs, and starts them all over again. By this time, I have picked up on some of the nuances of his vocal style and choices. I can predict which tones he will linger upon and which he will punch with extra emotion. I can pick up harmonies to compliment this or that note in every song, though I never fully realize the compilation by singing or humming. A part of me wishes that I could, but, of course, it is out of the question.

He stops to rest and to eat a can of pre-packaged spaghetti, which he produces, along with a fork, out of the bag. My stomach threatens to voice its jealousy and I pray it remains quiet. I can't eat anything. All I have are canned goods and they make far too much noise to open, so I watch as he wolfs down something I can only dream of tasting.

We walk for what seems forever through the junk lands. I drink the last of the water that I have collected. He stops once more to eat, drink, and rest, this time eating a less-desirable can of mushrooms.

Still, he is eating, and that is more than I can say about myself, so I'm still a little bitter.

The man takes long steps. Compared to the pace I have been setting for myself recently, this pace is brutal. Especially when trying to keep hidden, yet needing to keep him in sight, and when running on very low fuel. A few times, I come very close to just throwing up my hands and giving him up. Only, something inside won't let me. This is the only life form I've encountered for so long. If nothing else, I want to know how he keeps his hair so soft looking and where he found the pasta. Also, deep down in the recesses of my heart, I want to hear more songs and I don't want to be alone.

The man leads me to a little clearing in the junk, where a make-shift lean-to is made out of an old dining room table and a bookshelf. There is a mattress and some grungy blankets underneath the shelter. It must be his home. He sets the bag down inside the bookshelf and begins to empty his pockets, setting his butterfly knives, a pocket watch, a comb, and a wallet onto the next shelf up from the bag. On his left hand he wears a silver thumb ring and several thin brown bracelets decorate his wrist. These he removes as well, gingerly, and puts them with the rest of his belongings.

Next, causing me to blush, he takes off his clothes down to his boxers. He takes off his coat, and when he doesn't stop there, I turn away. I give him what I think is adequate time to do whatever he is doing, then quickly glance to make sure he hasn't disappeared. He has folded up his pants, shirt, and coat, and put them on the shelf, along with a pair of terribly unwashed socks and some very well worn-in tennis shoes.

I'm a little early in my peeking, though, as he is still up. He stands with his back to me and stretches his arms above his head, one hand holding onto the other wrist. He cracks his neck and flops into bed, throwing the blankets on over himself and rolling himself into a cocoon, as if sleeping on a dirty mattress in humanity's last days were completely normal and second nature to him.

I use the old trick Sights taught me, letting the unmistakable change of his breathing cue me that it is alright to move about. I open my pack and take out a can of tomatoes. Like all cans nowadays, the lid pops open with the help of a little tab. I fish out the pieces of what is arguably considered technically fruit with my fingers and greedily gobble them up. After they are gone, I drink the watery juice leftover in the can.

When my feast is gone, I find a nearby couch that has been broken almost literally in two, and lean up against it. The plan is to stay awake and listen for signs that the man has woken up.

However, as plans often go astray, I fall asleep, curled up against the couch.

Thirteen

"Friend?"

"Mmm?"

"What do you remember about the old world?"

"I remember traveling. I tried to see every inch of the world. I remember the jostle of the car as I drove around and the frustration I always got after about three hours of listening to music, when all songs started to blend together and I didn't want to listen to them anymore, but nothing else would keep me awake through the night. I remember going along highways where you would suddenly turn a corner or go over the peak of a hill and could see miles around you and, always, there would be little towns here and there that shimmered like lights on a Christmas tree.

"I would stop and sleep at the cheapest, crappiest little hotels. The kind where the showers wouldn't work and the sheets would be crispy and the wallpaper glue would be running down the walls. The TVs would only play porn, and I'd always bring my own pillow because half the time there wouldn't be one provided. But staying at *places like that was the only way I could ever afford to travel, and I'd rather have seen the world through the drafty windows of those hotels than spend my entire life caged in one pristine house in one pristine city."*

"Oh. Ok."

"What about you, Little Owl? What do you remember?"

"A lot of things."

"Such as...?"

"Snowball fights. The long, late-night drives my dad took us on sometimes up the mountain. Waiting for the school bus on crisp fall mornings. Baking bread with my grandmother when she was still alive, Doing photo shoots with my father. Bringing my mom breakfast in bed every Mother's Day. Playing pranks on the neighbor boys. Everything."

"Come here, Little Owl. Bring the light, come sit by me."

I set the light beside his mat and snuggle in next to him. He has one arm propped underneath his head to lift him up a bit, the other arm wraps around my shoulder in a comforting embrace. He readjusts the blankets so we are both under them and holds me close to him. I reach over and turn off the lantern.

"Once upon a time," he breathes near my ear, *"there was an old Irish farmer. He lived alone, just him and the prátai, and everyone laughed at him, for he frequently told anyone within earshot 'One day, I will live in the castle and the king will eat nothing but my potatoes.'"*

"That's a horrible accent."

"Shh... And the farmer paid them no heed. He kept growing his potatoes and experimenting with different ways to cook and flavor them. He spent every last penny on spices from all over the world, and for three years he cooked and broiled and baked and mashed until, one day, he took the perfect potato dish out of the oven."

"What was it?"

"Just listen... The oven had roasted the pepper-and-lemon potato wedges just the perfect golden color. The outside was crispy, while the inside melted in the farmer's mouth. He leapt in the air with joy! However, just to make sure he wasn't crazy, he invited the villagers to his house for a feast to try out the dish. Everyone loved the dish, from Jimmy, the school boy with the pickiest taste for food, to Moira, the old woman who lived on the shore and was renowned for preparing the best seafood chowder and brown bread for miles around, to even Padraig, the priest, who condemned

any rich flavored food on the grounds that the poor shall inherit the earth.

"So the farmer packed up his potatoes, spices, and his recipe, took up his walking stick, and walked the three day journey to the castle. He trimmed his beard and wore his best Sunday sweater and fisherman's cap to hide the spot where his soft, gray hair failed to grow, and knocked upon the castle door.

'Go away.' growled the guardsman.

'Please, sir,' replied the farmer in his most respectable tone. 'It has been me life's dream to create a dish of potatoes that is fit for his royal highness, the king. I have, not four days past, cooked such a meal, and have walked straight here that I may see the king enjoy it before I pass from this Earth into God's great heaven.'

"The guardsman turned him away again, but a servant girl who worked in the kitchen had overheard the farmer's desperate plea and simple wish. She sneaked him into the kitchen and told the cook his story, who also took pity on the poor farmer- for the cook could easily understand why any farmer should envy his job and wish for just one day to do what he did. So the cook agreed to give the farmer a chance.

"So the farmer took his prized potatoes- the last of the crop and the very best- and whispered a

*silent blessing over each one to cook well and
please the king. He drizzled them with cream and
butter, squeezed a drop or two of lemon (depending
on the size of the potato) and sprinkled salt, pepper,
and a dash of his secret ingredient upon them. He
cooked them for a while this way, then took them
out of the oven while they were still just crisp
enough to cut with ease, chopped them into wedges,
and then put more butter, lemon, and pepper, and a
dash of sugar on them.*

*"They cooked for a long while, filling the air
of the kitchen with a heavenly aroma. By the time
the potatoes were done, every single person in the
kitchen was salivating for a bite of the dish. Every
single person was denied. The potatoes were for the
king who could also smell them cooking, and who
sat at his feasting table excitedly awaiting his
luncheon.*

*"By and by, a young serving boy took the
plate of perfect potatoes to the king. Stomach
growling, eyes dilating, the king cut into the
potatoes and took a luxurious bite. The taste of such
a meal shamed the rest of the world. Every smell,
every taste the world had to offer was belittled by
the one bite of the farmer's potatoes. The king cried
a single tear as he swallowed, then dropped face-
first into the dish, dead. Some say that the beauty of
the dish swallowed his soul. Others insist that the
king was allergic to the pepper the farmer used.*

Whatever the truth, the king died with the first look of contentment anyone had ever seen him wear. The end."

"What happened to the farmer?"

"He died happy in the kitchen in the span between the completion of his dish and when the king tried it. Now go to sleep."

I laugh softly at that, which is a typical ending to one of Friend's tales. He turns on to his back and I follow, resting my head on his chest, with his left arm around me, and drift off.

I wake up with the memory of Friend still keeping me warm. It is the first morning I can remember, since surfacing, that I do not wake up shivering. When I remember where I am, I bolt upright, mentally scolding myself for sleeping when I should have been watching. Then I realize that I am covered in a blanket.

I don't know how to react. I am really tempted to just call this a success and curl back up into sleep. Instead, I look around the edge of the couch. The man is still asleep, this time coiled up within his patchwork coat. Only a few ringlets of his hair and the very tips of his toes are visible. I relax a little bit, and fall back to eat some breakfast.

Today's meal consists of Mandarin oranges, which have always been a favorite of mine. After I've finished them, I gather up the blanket and go toward the man. After all this time of slinking in shadows and from cover to cover, it feels extremely odd to cross the open space, knowing that, at any moment, he could open his eyes and see me.

I tread silently. He doesn't stir when I drape the blanket over him and pull it up around his shoulders. I watch him for a while. I know I probably shouldn't. I'm putting myself in more risk than I need to, but it has been so long since I've been so close to a sleeping figure. We are vulnerable when we sleep, fragile even, and even now, if I chose to, I could kill him. I could slit his throat with my grandfather's knife or rob him of his supplies so that he slowly starves to death while I eat like a king.

Or, I could take his knives. Without them, he would be severely disabled in the confrontation that is sure to take place shortly. My gut says these knives mean a lot to him and, by taking them, I could take control of this situation. I could control him. I pick up one of the knives, flip it open and examine it. It is gorgeous and gleaming with potential. I close it and put it back. After all, he could have taken my life, my supplies, my weapon, and he didn't. Also, what would I do with a life in my control?

The man turns over and accepts the blanket over his head, kicking a bit to get the blanket under

his feet. I step back in case he wakes. He doesn't.
He just kicks and kicks until I roll my eyes and
arrange the blanket the way he's trying- failing- to
get it. He stops thrashing about and sleeps on.

Now that I've completely overstepped my
boundaries with this man to whom I've not even
spoken, I don't know what to do. I can't stay here,
to watch and wait for him to wake and address me.
No, I will do what I always do. I will find some
food and move on. I have lingered here long
enough. I gather my bag and am about to move out
when a voice halts me in my step.

"Wait." The man, fully groggy and slurring
his attempt at speech, says to me "Don't go.
Please."

I turn around. The man is standing, with his
coat wrapped around his waist, trying for modesty.
He wipes at his eyes with the hand that isn't holding
his coat and then runs it through his hair to push his
curls out of his face. They bounce back with
charming ferocity, determined to remain a mussed
terror for the man. I do what he has asked; I wait.

"Um."

"Go ahead, get dressed." I suggest, and point
to the couch. "I'll be there."

He nods, brows furrowed apologetically. I
give him a gentle smile and turn away. I hear a
commotion and a little bit of swearing under his

breath as he struggles with his clothing. He must be a heavy sleeper.

It doesn't take him too long before he knocks at the couch. I stand up and face him. His hair is still comically uncontrolled, but the rest of him has been assembled. We stare at each other, taking each other in without leaving each other's eyes. I'm not sure why we do this. I've been following him long enough that there is nothing about him that shocks me, while he must have had all the time in the world to take me in while I slept. I blush a little at that thought, which is his cue to speak.

"Hello."

Not the most promising start, but then again, what do you say to the only other person on Earth?

"Hello." I reply, giving him control of this conversation, since he was the one who insisted it take place.

"Have you been following me?"

"Yes."

"For how long?"

I hesitate, not really knowing how to measure the time. I choose not to mention the skeletons.

"Since the morning of the last wake-span."

He nods, than regains my gaze in a direct gaze.

"Why?"

I shrug, remembering what Friend always told me when he did not want to answer that question. "Why did the scorpion sting the hippo?"

He looks confused, so I explain the story- how the scorpion wished to cross the river on the hippo's back, but the hippo knew to grant such a favor was a death wish. The scorpion promised not to sting and pleaded so ardently that the hippo finally gave in. Halfway across the river, the scorpion stung the hippo because it was in his nature to do so, and they both drowned.

The man tosses his head, like a young stallion, trying again to rid himself of his irritating bed-head.

"So it is your nature to follow me," the man says slowly. "and kill us both."

I smile. "Yeah. Halfway across the river."

"Ok." He returns my smile with a very cheeky one of his own, "Just so I've been warned."

"You have."

"So who are you? What's your name?"

I'm caught off guard. No one asks for a name anymore. I'm put on the defensive and realize how familiar our conversation has been. With the need to put distance back in its proper place between us, I overlook the question and change the subject.

"Where does this trail lead?" I walk around him and look around at his little dwelling and the junk that shelters it from view. He must travel this way often, or live here, yet the trail goes on further.

The man glances sharply down the trail and then returns his attention to me, scrutinizing me. Perhaps there is a deep, dark secret at the end of the path with which he does not trust me. Fair enough, I don't ask for anyone's confession.

"I come from a place far from here, where nothing grows," I tell him, trying to offer amends for whatever I have done to offend him, "I had no idea there was such a place as this."

He relaxes his jaw ever so slightly.

"You're from across the Storm Lands?"

More names. If by Storm Lands he means the cities that have been destroyed by the wind storms, then yes. I shrug, dropping my gaze to the ground.

"I honestly don't know. Until last wake-span I did not know other lands existed, much less had names. I didn't even know there was anyone around to name them." My eyes rise to meet his. "Then I saw you."

He is concerned. I have chosen my words and implications carefully, mostly to gauge his reaction. Names imply people; groups of people. The ease with which he talks to me and the fact that he wasn't surprised to see me- that I am aware of- indicates he knows there are people, perhaps has seen them, perhaps he has spoken to them. However, his secrecy with the trail makes me think he does not want me to know there are others.

"You're alone?"

There it is. He's not alone. What's more, he expects me to have company as well. I look around at the junk and see, for the first time, the potential for unlimited hiding spots. This is the perfect place for an ambush. My stomach lurches. I should have taken the knives when I had the chance.

"You aren't alone?" I ask, not taking my eyes off my surroundings.

Out of my peripherals, I see the man fold his arms and look at me for a long, contemplative moment. He plays with something up his sleeve. I catch a glint of rainbow; his knives. I quickly draw my grandfather's knife from its hiding place and plant my feet, preparing for a fight that I know I cannot win. He responds with deadly speed, drawing both knives out of his sleeves, flipping them open and showing off his skill before coming to ready position.

"Let me guess," I snap, "a gentlemanly sense of propriety compelled you to keep me warm last night so I could give you a fair fight today."

"Why didn't you kill me this morning, when *you* had the chance?" He responds.

I lower my weapon, eyes hard set on the human face before me. It is hard to reign in my instincts, which cannot ignore his threats. Here he is- all the makings of a human being: eyes, breath, body, voice, someone responsive, someone vulnerable, someone warm. He had appeared so suddenly when I had known with absolute certainty that I would never see another life again. I could never make him understand how much it means to me that someone else exists.

"You are the first living thing I've seen in…" I sheathe my grandfather's knife, breathing through the shaking fear of my vulnerability. "I understand if you want to kill me- protect you, protect yours- I get it. But I come from the land of death and the dead have haunted me every step of my journey. I have no wish to witness death ever again."

I swallow the catch in my throat. He drops his knives and takes a step, reaching for me, something tender and hungry in his eyes. I flinch, backing away until he realizes I will keep distance between us. I may not want him dead, that doesn't mean I want him close.

The man picks up his knives and puts them away. He looks at me with an unreadable expression that somehow terrifies me more than the threat that has just passed. I hate myself for what has just happened. I should never have come here after him. There are no heroes. *I do not care how badly you want there to be, heart, there are no heroes. You best just fade away here and now.*

"You aren't alone, you know." The man says, tossing me a full, unopened bottle of water. I catch it and twist off the cap with one fluid movement. He continues: "There are others who survived the storms. I'm just one more. Most live in clumps here and there throughout the Ruins. Uh, that's this place. It is said the winds pushed everything until they met each other here and, since they could not overpower each other, here is where everything stayed."

The man gesticulates as he talks, a nervous habit, one he did not display until now. His explanation makes sense. A person could live quite happily in this land of endless resources. Towns could even flourish here, provided some system of government and structure could be agreed upon. I say nothing in return. I've already done enough damage for the day with what I've said. I need my guard to return now and stay forever.

I want to ask if he lives here, but I'm pretty sure I know the answer. These trails through the ruins are like those of an ant hill: they twist and turn, but lead to the main cavern of dwelling. This path is just one of many, created to lead out in case of emergencies and for the purposes of allowing workers to scavenge supplies for the rest of the camp. The man with the patched coat lives here, making sure it is guarded. Ensuring that threats, like me, or whoever he thought I was, stay away from the rest of the people. The insignia he wears on his chest that I cannot place probably marks his rank or class or even the group of people to which he belongs.

I may have walked in isolation this entire time, but he has never even taken a step alone. He has a home and, probably, a family. Yes, there are people in the world again, yet I am as alone as ever, and I will never belong to a civilization ever again. I am ruin and destruction and the woman who survives even herself.

"Who are you?" The man insists gently. Has he been watching me the whole time? There is no point in lying now.

"I come from the Underground, where my family and I fled during the storms. It was a tomb that consumed everyone. Except me. I survived on my own, crawled out, on some false ambition that my life could help humanity somehow. Or, at least, make some sense of their deaths. The Surface offered little more than the Underground could, but I journeyed on. I'm not sure what I was looking for. You, I guess. But I see I'm not really needed, so I think I better go. Don't ask where, I don't know. It doesn't really matter. Thank you for everything."

This, apparently, does not sit well with him. His expression turns dark.

"You could stay here." He offers.

"No." I offer a smile in return. "I have to keep moving or the ghosts will catch up. Thank you though."

"I don't mind, you know."

"What?"

His head is downcast, yet he still meets my eyes as he talks. He is very brave that way.

"Going to the middle of the river with you. Even if we drown."

He flashes a smile at me. I cannot tell if he is mocking me.

"I don't understand."

He has already begun to look around the junk for hidden supplies: a few cans of food under an old tire, a bottle of water in the drawer of a dresser, extra clothing from I'm not sure where.

"I've heard some of the gathering talk about a forest. It somehow survived the storms. I've always wanted to see it. Maybe it's enchanted, I don't know, but it seems to me that if you are looking for peace from your past that you don't go to somewhere ravaged by that same past. You go to a place that thrived despite it all."

An excited chatter begins to form in my mind followed by the pounding of my heart. He is coming with me. I won't be alone. I am about to embark on a quest to find an enchanted forest accompanied by a magician. I think I am about to have an adventure.

He throws the supplies in his bag, filling it up, and then asks for my backpack. I chuck it at him. As he catches it by one strap, something falls to the ground. It is my father's camera. I had forgotten its existence. He picks it up, examines it, and briskly moves through the waist-high junk to a very specific location. There is a small, wooden box that he opens, grabs something from, and closes again, replacing it in its hidden spot. He puts two batteries into the camera and flips it on.

I watch, stunned, as the light from the digital display flickers across his fine-featured face. He goes through every picture, smiling occasionally.

When he sees the last few pictures, his face goes gray and he turns it off. I'm biting my lip, frozen, when he looks back at me. He skips back to me and throws an arm around me and takes a picture of us. Winking, he hands the camera to me.

Now, when I turn on the camera, I do not automatically see the last thing my father and sister saw before they died. There are no black clouds or destructive winds staring at me. I am not facing the funnel clouds, the lightning, or the hail that destroyed our lives forever. Those pictures are still there, but now I have to choose to look at them. Now, the automatic picture that appears is one of a new start.

I look at it. How easily his arm embraces me, how charming his smile, as if we are close friends. I am not smiling. I am looking at him with surprise, and to my deepest and fullest regret, longing.

"How is it? Acceptable?" He asks playfully as he fills my pack.

No. This is anything but acceptable.

"It's great."

I shut off the camera, take out the batteries, and throw them aside.

Fourteen

Despite the friendly conversation at our departure, we fall silent as strangers as soon as we set out. The man, who is considerably taller than I am, and who knows this trail far better than I do, travels a lot quicker than I. He takes long, silent strides that I try- and fail- to master. After a while, I become out of breath and he notices how much slower it is to effectively navigate the narrow trail in combat boots. He slows.

As he slows, just to make sure I know he's trying to be considerate, he begins to talk to me, weaving elaborate stories about the group of people with whom he has lived since the storms. They call themselves the Gathering and the Ruins are set up the way I imagined them. The Gathering is made up of humans who survived the storms in shelters that were not a part of the Underground. After the bulk of the storms, they emerged, found each other, and gathered at the Ruins to rebuild their lives.

There are just about a hundred people in the Gathering, which is larger than any other group of people that have been reported since the storms. Their structure is council-based. They have ten "families" of ten people, one of whom represents the family in the council. Each family, marked by the insignia upon their clothing, has one council member: one gatherer who, as their name suggests, gathers supplies from the Ruins for the family; two craftspeople, who make and fix everything from houses to clothing to the musical instruments that the people use at festivities; two technicians to invent and create efficient ways of obtaining electricity, plumbing, and weaponry; and the remaining four have jobs pertinent to the talents they have to offer. Often, the remaining four are young adults, children, or elderly civilians who end up doing menial work or training in specific tasks.

It is interesting, when the man with the patched coat talks about the Gathering, he does so with detachment, as if he were not attached or a part of the community. I don't bring it up. I make a point to never ask questions for which I am not prepared to hear the answer. I pretend, instead, that he has joined the Gathering too late to be assigned a family, and is a rouge knight that protects the Gathering, but can never, truly, be a part of it. I cannot help but wonder, however, if his detachment has anything to do with his eagerness to join my journey.

The more he talks, the more he smiles, which has a strange, shy way of curving up on one side more than the other. He describes in great lengths and proud gesticulation how the Gathering is creative as well as resourceful in their improvised settlement. The houses, which might be made of a couch as one wall and a car on the other, are always cleaned and decorated at all times by literary wallpaper made from the select few pages of books not destroyed by the rain or hail or tiled with shards of broken things with specific color patterns or textures.

"There is one old woman, Fatima, who is a master at making her hovel a home. Each bedroom, which generally holds two or three people, reflects the personality of the people who live there. And, of course, it all depends on what the gatherers bring back. Fatima is notorious for making her gatherers sleep outside if they don't bring her back the exact right thing, you know? Darris has been kicked out so many times, poor bastard, he never knows what to get!"

The man laughs with a chuckle that is placed in the back of his throat. I trail my hand beside me on the leg of an extravagant bedpost. His laugh makes me smile instinctively. I have grown more at-ease with patched-coat as we've been traveling. Once he decides to talk, he is good company.

"Darris used to be a computer programmer. He's really good at finding useful things, but he doesn't have an imaginative bone in his body."

"What were you? Before everything…"

He looks back at me with a surprisingly blank expression, meeting my eyes fleetingly before looking down at the steps that I am taking. His mouth parts slightly, a corner of it twitching upward briefly. I think I've offended him. I certainly didn't mean to ask the question, it just slipped out before I thought about it. He faces ahead again before he answers me.

"I wasn't really much of anything: a high school student with too much time on my hands. I was going to be a- was going to study biology. I did a summer internship at a local zoo and fell in love with the idea of raising and training all the exotic animals. There is a beauty in the way the muscles of big cats move, how Tamarins glide from tree to tree, the looks a sloth will give you… it was, well, magic. I mean, I cleaned a lot of animal poop, I never got to actually work with the animals, but I always wanted to."

"I'm sorry."

He shrugs and passes a smile my way.

"What about you?" He asks.

"I wanted to be a fashion designer." I lie, letting the first tale that comes to my mind- inspired by his coat- slip off of my forked tongue. Well, why not? Someone must have wanted to design clothing before the art was rendered useless by bad weather, and the lie is a lot more satisfying than the truth of my undeclared life.

He beams, realizing I'm eyeing his coat, and turns to face me. I hate him for being able to walk backwards through this junkyard maze when it takes so much concentration for me to just maneuver my way through it. It's like walking through a child's room- they know exactly where to step, yet I stumble and trip over every toy strewn across the floor.

"Lori was studying fashion too. She made this for me. It was a birthday present slash final project for her home-ec class. It wasn't quite finished for my birthday, but she gave it to me anyway."

"It's beautiful."

"Right? She used to have a box just filled with leftover scraps of fabric color-coordinated by her sources of inspiration. These were all from her Van Gogh Self Portrait box."

"Huh. I could see that, actually. That's great."

"I love it." A sudden shadow of sorrow crosses his face. His expression reveals more than I wish to know about the fate of the girl named Lori. We fall silent again as I do not know how to comfort him.

We stop for lunch and each contribute a can of provisions, allowing us the invaluable variety of both pre-packaged pasta and pre-packaged beans. Patched-coat surprises me with a little packet of powered flavoring, which makes the stale water we've brought taste like watered-down lemonade. It is a sweet gesture.

"Well," he sighs near the end of our rest, "we are going to have to veer off the trail soon."

Oh great. I can't even navigate through a ready-made trail and now we get to wander free-for-all through the junk? I make an off-hand comment along that same line of thought which causes him to throw his head back and laugh.

"Don't worry," he grins, touching my forehead lightly with two fingers. "I'll be there to hold your hand the entire way."

I return his smile with a mock-hurt look which melts away of its own accord into a smile. We both drop each other's gaze at the same time. I am still beaming privately when we decide to move out. It is time to brave the Ruins.

Trudging through the endless piles of garbage and treasures really isn't as bad as I thought it would be. I originally pictured Patches leaping on top everything like that first day that I saw him while I half-stumbled, half-swam through it all. This isn't entirely accurate. Patches is having almost as much difficulty as I am wading through the miles of material possessions.

This is a ridiculous amount of stuff, and almost all of it is garbage. My sister used to collect and save every little thing, the little dragon, but even she would have a conniption at this mess! Eventually I just have to accept the priceless with the worthless underfoot and pretend that every crunch is just a piece of already-broken glass or garbage. It is just not practical to watch every step or try to scoot things around as I step to avoid breakables.

It is surprisingly warm here, warmer than the Storm Lands obviously, but also warmer than the trail. Maybe it is due to the fact that everything here is packed so tightly against each other, or maybe I am just using more energy, and therefore, keeping myself temperate. When I start to sweat, I take off my jacket and tie it around my backpack. It's been long enough since I have been able to wash, I don't want to push my luck with how odorous I have become, especially traveling with someone who doesn't seem to ever even glisten. How is that even possible? The man is wearing a thermo shirt and a coat! He disgusts me sometimes.

Somewhere along the way, his coat gets caught on a sliver of wood jutting out from a large chunk of wall. Before I can call out to him to stop a moment, there is a heart-wrenching ripping sound. The damage is extensive- at least three of the patches are torn. However, most of it is just that the seams wouldn't hold, so it should be able to be fixed pretty easily provided he has packed a sewing kit.

We have. Patches made sure of that, hiding it in my backpack. I am exhausted. So, while he sits precariously perched on the back of a recliner, clumsily stitching away at his memory, I brush the dust and pieces of plastic and metal from the seat of the chair, curl up, and fall asleep at his feet. He doesn't wake me, but begins to sing a little to himself after he's finished with his mending. I should ask where he learned those songs, they are very good...

When I wake, Patches is stretched out on an uncomfortable-looking door a few feet away. The hairs on my bare arms are raised, as if I've caught a chill while I slept, but I am not cold at all. I look across the land of Ruins, the inevitable proof that human beings waste and want too much. Hovering above the world's biggest hoard is the figure of a person, all covered in shadow.

I have not seen the Thunderbourne since it almost touched me. I was almost beginning to think that this had all been a nightmare. I sigh and give the creature an unenergetic wave. It responds by locking onto my eyes and coming towards me at an alarming rate. I shake Patches awake.

"What is it?" He groans. "I let you sleep…"

"It's late." We both know I have no way of knowing that. "We should go."

My tone does not allow for argument, so he stretches, rolls over, and slowly sits up. I stare down at him impatiently.

"Why the rush?"

"I just think we should keep moving is all."

When I look around again, the Thunderbourne is nowhere to be seen. Somehow this is more unsettling than being able to see it. I pick up Patches' bag and begin to scoot around boxes and toy trains, and… a gun? I pick it up. It is almost fully loaded.

Patches is bent over, scratching his scalp, trying to use gravity to rid himself of his bed-head. While he is not looking, I slip grandfather's knife out of its place on my hip and find it a new home next to my ankle in my boots, wrapped up in socks so it does not accidentally cut my foot. The gun goes in the sheath. It fits, but barely, and I have to tie my jacket around my waist instead of my pack to hide it.

What funny creatures, humans, to place faith in such a little thing as a gun. In the scheme of things, especially against demons and shadows like the Thunderbourne, it is little more than a noisemaker and security blanket. At least, last time I tried to use a gun against them it didn't do much. Then again, I couldn't see much. Maybe it killed them all and turned them all to shadow-dust.

The panic is fresh in me now, reanimated with vivid ferocity from that night in the Underground. No, I have a sinking feeling that the gun did absolutely nothing against our hunters. The feeling rolls around in my gut as Patches takes a lifetime to get up and going. At least I am able to convince him to eat his breakfast on the road.

Fifteen

As tradition seems to dictate, we spend the first chunk of our time this wake-span in silent trudgery. The Ruins here are compiled mostly of smaller things. There is a plethora of children's toys, collectibles with half-faces or chipped edges, umbrellas and canes, and so many, many books damaged beyond repair or remembrance.

We come across a clearing that is set up like a tiny tea party. Someone has laid down a blanket over the broken debris and lined up hundreds of tea cups and their mismatched saucers. The teapots are set on stacks of books around the edge of the picnic. It is oddly poetic and eerie at the same time.

We avoid walking on the blanket as if it were a faerie ring waiting to spirit us away. I do, however, lift one of the tea pot lids as we pass. There is liquid inside it. Patched-coat brings a flashlight over to me and shines it over my shoulder. The "tea" is very watery and shining bright green. I pick up the white teapot and lean it towards me. There is a clink as a piece of green glass shifts across the bottom of the teapot and falls against the ceramic side.

The other teapots all hold shards of different colored glass in them as well, making the water appear exotic and bright. Something about this pseudo-happy display leaves me shaken and upset. Somewhere inside me an image rises of someone drinking water and glass, the green glass turning the water red as it slices open the inside of someone's throat. I reset the dishes and stumble through the Ruins with a new-found determination to find a place beyond all of this distortion and destruction.

Patches watches me carefully. I suppose my behavior has been weird. I try to lighten the mood by finding something around us to comment on. A conversation would be a nice transition from the creepy morning into a more pleasant afternoon. Unfortunately mostly everything in this section is garbage, so all I get out is an old film reference or two.

"What a lovely smell you've discovered."

He chuckles, but doesn't seem very responsive. So, after a few failed attempts at communication, I leave him alone. I've somehow managed to walk in front, however I don't know the way, so I slow down to let him pass me. He doesn't. He responds by slowing down as well and giving me a strange look when I glance at him.

I don't understand. Does he think I am going to run away? I'm not going to slip away unexpectedly into the garbage. Why would I? I glance back a second time. This time, Patches is also looking back, a hand clutched at something in his pocket.

Oh. It hits me harshly. There is something following us, Thunderbourne or human. He is placing himself between me and the threat. He is trying to protect me. I'm a little ashamed and surprisingly offended. I never asked him to risk himself for me. I've gotten this far, he does not have to fight my battles for me. He is not my hero.

Yet, wasn't it just this morning that, when threatened, I ran to him? When the Thunderbourne approached, I turned my tail and went to him, waking him from what was probably a much-needed sleep because I was frightened. What am I doing, anyway? This man left his home and his family for me. I have no one waiting for my return, and he does. Why did I ever let him come with me? Surely my loneliness is a worthy price of his safe reunion with those he cares for and who care for him.

I should have led the Thunderbourne away from him this morning. I should have let him go back. He smiles at me. Apparently I've unconsciously sought out his face over my shoulder. I smile in return, though I do not doubt he notices its weakness.

"Are you ok?" He asks gently. I love how I'm a master of self control except when I most want its shielding properties.

"I'm fine." I whisper, using an old lie. "Just a little tired."

"Well if someone wouldn't have insisted we leave so dang early…"

I raise an eyebrow at him and find a twinkle in his eye that comforts me. The feeling that I'm selfishly leading him to his doom doesn't really go away, but it is decreased by his relaxed expression and the quiet mischief shining in the way he inclines his head slightly to the left.

"By the way," I say dryly. "I have no idea where I'm going. I'm just guessing I'm leading us the correct way."

"You're doing just fine."

"Good. Because we wanted to find the world's biggest garbage can, right?"

He laughs.

"What else would we want to find?"

I can't help but smile as we continue on. The good mood we've established makes me a little more ecstatic than I think I should be, but I can probably count on one hand the times I've been giddy since Friend died. Screw it, I want to be happy. Why does being happy feel so wrong?

I choose to ignore my conscience and am still smiling to myself when we sit down for lunch. We only share one can of vegetables, corn of all things, because the smell of the garbage is overpowering enough that after a few bites neither of us has much of a stomach. We spend our break holding our breath- him by covering his nose with his sleeve, me by wrapping my scarf around my face- and trying not to giggle when we catch each other's eyes. The whole scene is ridiculous.

The rest of our journey this wake-span is spent trying desperately to get out of garbage-land. The overpowering stench of rotten food intensifies even as we try to elude it. Then, suddenly, the garbage at our feet clears away. There is a moment right before the peak of a small hill where we can walk freely.

I nudge the dry dirt of the Ruins with my toes and watch it formulate into a brown cloud. The wind makes the peak cold with no junk to shelter us. I almost put my coat back on until I remember that it is hiding the gun. I have no way of knowing whether or not Patches has been watching me closely enough to know my weaponry, but I don't want to risk it. I don't know why, but I don't want him to know that I have it.

I look at the tall, gracefully lanky companion of mine. The wind is playing terror with his hair, and he is laughing at it. He is so changeable. One moment he's terrifying and threatening, a man I would not cross for all the honor of the world. The next he's just a boy, laughing at the wind and clumsily stabbing at his pretty coat with a needle he does not know how to use. Does he have a family in the Gathering, or did he just make it up the way that I made up stories about who I am?

I know how easy it is to lie. I was born and bred for deceit. Lying is what protects me: it is my shield. It is the ice that keeps my heart from beating on fire and burning up everything I am. No one gets near my heart anymore. The lies make sure of it.

If I can lie, so can he. What if he killed the Gathering, or even made them all up? He obviously does not know where we are going, so why take me here? His decision to accompany me came out of nowhere and runs against every story he's told me thus far. He is charming and beautiful and deadly, and the decision to claim and hide my new gun was not to arm me against the Thunderbourne, but him.

I leave my coat around my waist and grip my scarf to me like a shawl. Why is every word, every action, and even every laugh an exploration in right and wrong? I hate how complicated everything is. I wish Friend were here to tell me what to do. Of course, even he never really told me who he was.

Even the man with whom I was the most honest, the most open, and the most vulnerable, never really gave me reason to care for him the way I did.

No, that's not true. He was honest with me. At least, I chose to trust him. I may not have known who Friend was before finding me, but I have to believe I did know who he was when he was with me. Patches is different. Even the earnest look in his eyes is half-muted by some other obscure intent. The light in him is very easily changed into darkness.

I've blinked and the shade has re-emerged on Patches face. He has passed the crest of the hill and is looking down on the sight of a new horror. The wind shifts and brings me a clue of what is below. I feel the blood drain away from my head, the nausea that spins from my gut to my temples. I fall to my knees as I come to the crest. Stretching out below us, as far as the eye can see, are bodies.

"Please." I manage between the broken breaths that follow my gagging. "Let's find another way."

The valley is littered with broken, twisted, and rotting corpses. Some seem remarkably fresh, others are little more than a bone or two among the dust. Remembering the skeletons I found the day I met Patches, I am glad I cannot see their faces clearly. Patches tears his eyes away from the scene and does not look back. He walks back down the hill. I stumble forward, half-crawling as I struggle to my feet after him.

"I am sorry." Patches says darkly without facing me.

"For what?" I catch up to him and do my best to stay by his side. "You didn't do this."

He shakes his head and does not answer. Fine, keep your secrets. It's not like I need any more anyway. I don't fall behind him. I want him to know that this isn't something he needs to keep from me. I am an equal witness to the valley of the shadow of death and I fear no evil. Except what I fear from him.

I don't know if Patches is going to draw his knives and kill me, leave me, or try to protect me from whatever this is. I am getting very tired of his inconsistencies. I wish he'd pick a role to try to fill and stick with it. I fall out of step with him and give up, letting him tromp ahead back into the land of garbage. Controlling my urge to branch off and find my own way, I follow sullenly behind.

Time passes unremarkably. I am happy when it is time to stop for rest. I have waited until Patches decides he is too weary to go on, which is a great deal farther than I would have liked, but I'm not going to show any weakness right now. Let him think that I could go on farther. Let him think I am stronger than I am.

There are no couches or chairs or mattresses nearby. Just bags and piles of trash. I stand, watching Patches with exhaustion, but refusing to show the full extent of my weariness until he is lost in dreams. After a while, he lies down and turns his back to me, using his coat as a blanket-cocoon. I choose what I think is a corner less odiferous than the others, quite a distance away from Patches and plop my backpack down. I hide the gun in the backpack so I'm not sleeping on it and cover myself with my coat, pulling it up over my head.

Despite the length and hardship of the wake-span's journey, it is difficult to sleep. I feel a rising in my chest that I know will not bring anything good. At least I can keep the waterworks at bay until Patches' breathing slows. The salt burns my bloodshot eyes, and I feel like I need to scream. I stuff the scarf against my face and exhale with all the strength of a scream. I do not engage my voice box, though, so it is relatively silent. I do this again and again until I can no longer feel my lips. Soon, my whole face is tingling. I accept the numbness and let myself slip into slumber.

Sixteen

I am walking along a great and endless beach, a voluminous cloud lingering over the water ready to burst. There are a handful of people around me, dressed in ancient styles of beachwear. There are women in large hats and swimsuits that make them look like early Barbie dolls and children and men who follow them in tank suit swimwear and sunglasses.

There is a wolf on the beach, which no one else sees, who is endlessly shifting from a figure robed in gray, black, and brown cloths and back to biting teeth and yellow canine eyes. I turn and begin to run. The sand slows me down and I cannot get very far, but I scream and scream that the Storm Gods are coming. No one heeds my warning. They do not even see me.

The cloud explodes into a section of the beach before me. When the spiraling winds clear and the particles of sand settle around the newly-created crater, I find myself looking at a man with glowing white skin, spiky blue hair, and a very impressive suit of black armor with a cape that mirrors the colors and attitude of the wolf-demon.

The man fixes my gaze with storm-cloud gray eyes. He dismisses me almost instantly. I am neither a threat nor a treat for this monster, this Storm God.

He turns his attention to the rest of the humans and I watch, helplessly, as he picks a victim. The Storm God's eyes grow wide and lusting. He produces a terrifying war hammer in one hand, almost as tall and massive as he is. The Storm God approaches his target, a strong looking man with a defined jaw line and large green eyes, wearing the tattered garments of the Underground. The Storm God comes within inches of the man, and with only a look, disarms the man completely. The hand which held the war hammer gently caresses the man's neck up from his shoulder to the tip of his chin. He draws the man in and kisses him.

When the Storm God draws away, the man is left with his own set of jade eyes and hungering demeanor. This man finds a beautiful woman to attack, who chooses her prey, and they move through the entire beach this way until everyone is a Thunderbourne- except the children who disappear beneath the waves and me. The last to turn is a man whose toned, dark body is free from the restraints of a shirt.

He looks up to the shore where a new group of people are flooding onto the beach, unaware of any danger. The rest of the Thunderbourne are nowhere to be found, so I concentrate on this heartbreakingly beautiful demon. He seems to see through me. I have to gain his attention somehow. Not knowing what else to do, I strip out of my clothes.

This catches his attention. I lock onto his eyes and hold them as I walk towards the sea. The water is brutally cold, but I force myself not to shiver. The demon follows me into the sea, and when it is deep enough that only my shoulders rise like shaking white islands out of the ocean, he catches up to me.

He grabs my shoulders and pulls me so very closely. I search his eyes. I am not afraid. My hands cup his face, savoring the feeling of his soft, smooth skin. I take one more look into his deep eyes, flickering between brown like those of someone I once loved and lightning-green, and then I close myself to the world. I shut my eyes and press my slightly-parted lips against his, flicking my tongue to taste the salt water on his lips, then continue with the kiss. To my surprise, he moves his head ever so slightly away from me.

"Wait." He whispers to me softer than the feel of the water on my skin. "What happens next? I want to be free."

I can't move. I'm paralyzed against his body, wrapped within something I cannot understand. I feel him pulling me underwater, but I cannot even move to cry out or take a breath. He has moved my left leg so that it is bent at his hip, so he can maneuver the water. He surfaces often enough that I do not risk drowning. Even still, I am frightened beyond belief, panicked by my inability to move away from the Thunderbourne.

Suddenly, we are out of the water and he is setting me down onto the sand. I am able to move enough to attempt covering myself with my arms, though my eyes and voice still are frozen shut and still. The Thunderbourne leans over and brushes my cheekbone as he whispers one final time in my ear.

"Save me."

I wake with too many forces against me to allow me the luxury of movement. It is cold and raining. The memory of yesterday, mixed with the memory of the dream, leaves me upset as well as miserable from the chill. Also, to top it all off, my head and eyes are unbalanced and sore from crying myself to sleep.

I manage to uncurl a little, stretching out and throwing myself to my other side and see that Patches is already awake. Good. Because what I really needed this morning was someone I mistrust seeing me at my weakest. I bury my head in the balled up scarf which serves as a makeshift pillow and try to inconspicuously wipe away any sign or mark of last night's tears.

I know my eyes are still puffy. I can feel them itch and burn, and I more than slightly wish I could claw them out just for the sake of not having to explain myself to Patches. I defy the gravitational pull that comes specifically from my pounding brain and sit up. Running my fingers through my hair, I realize that it has come to that frustrating length where it decides to do whatever it wants. Thankfully it only takes the rain a moment to soak through it and flatten it down.

Patches is just finishing a breakfast can of packaged meat product. Between that and the moist smell of garbage, I decide to skip eating this time around. He watches me as I locate my bag. It isn't where I left it last night. Either I was thrashing about in my sleep and kicked it or Patches moved it. I don't like the implications of either thought.

"Today promises to be pleasant." I mutter as I take off my jacket and throw on my pack.

"As long as it is better than yesterday," he replies as I replace my jacket. "we'll survive."

By the time we stop for lunch, the rain has drifted away, lingering only in that slight metallic smell of approaching or depreciating rain. After that, Patches' mood seems to lighten a bit. He starts humming to himself. I recognize the melody from his repertoire of songs. I almost ask him about the songs, but think better of it. I scrounge my pack for food, letting him alone to his own thoughts and melodies.

"Do you like peas?" I ask when I come across the vile can in my pack.

"What?"

"Peas. I hate them, but I have a can. You want them?"

He hesitates, then accepts the bane of my existence when it comes to food stuffs. In return, he gives me the gift of pasta.

"Good. Trade." He quotes at me, making me smile.

We are both very tired of walking. We leave the garbage behind eventually, even though we're not exactly back-tracking. We avoid the Valley of Death and do not come across the Glass-Eater's tea party. The next section we pass through is filled with what seems like craft store supplies and toys. I wonder what caused these sections to separate. Are there people or creatures living here who make it their life's purpose to sort out the shit that outlived humanity?

The heaps of junk make jagged hills, filled with everything that could make a person trip, fall, and die. Strings seem to wrap themselves around my ankles out of nowhere. There are little fuzzies from some cotton-y crafting thing flying through the air, ensuring perpetual coughing. Even Patches, with his inhuman grace, stumbles and ducks and trips.

There's a pile of wooden 2x4s that reach out and grab Patches' coat. It tears without him knowing, and a large section of it continues to unravel. When I see it, I try to catch up to unhook it, but don't get there fast enough.

"Patches. Wait a second- your coat." I call out. He stops and turns, tearing it one more time before he realizes what is going on. For the first time, however, his focus is not on his coat, despite the extent of the damage.

"What did you call me?" he inquires quietly as he gathers the broken bits of his hem.

"Um, Patches? Because of, you know, your coat."

"Yeah?" He shakes his head. "I thought you didn't believe in names."

"I don't."

"Oh ok, so what did you call me?"

"It's not a name." I explain "It's a feature. I can't just call you 'man' or 'him'; it's just a defining feature. That's all."

He nods, rolling his eyes.

"So what *am* I supposed to call you? If not 'girl' and not your name?"

I'm not sure I like the expression he uses to look at me. I look around and pick up the first thing I can find, a plastic tiara, and put it on my head.

"Call me 'queen of the ruins' or 'your highness.' And while you're at it, don't forget to bow and do everything I say, knight of the patched coat."

He grins at me, fighting the urge to laugh. I try and look as proud as I can, lifting an arm to pompously wave at the air. We have a good, long moment of pretending and laughing.

"No, but seriously. What can I call you?" He says after flicking the tiara off my head. I shrug.

"Call me whatever you want- Trip, Blunder, Waste-of-time, whatever you think is applicable."

He casts me another long look that is hard to accept.

"Miracle." He says with finality.

"What?"

"You're the girl who came up from the Underground. No one does that. You're a miracle."

It is my turn to give him an odd look. He smirks nervously and looks down, away from my scrutiny. I wonder if I've been too rash in my assumptions about this man.

"Let's move out." I suggest softly and begin to walk away. I know that he takes a moment to take off his coat and put it in his bag, so I walk slowly. Yet I do walk. I remember that to keep moving is my utmost priority. I can't stop to look back, not even for friendship. Not even for someone who calls me a miracle.

Seventeen

For a period of time the only communication we have comes when whoever is leading casts a backwards glance. Always, these looks mean more than I can comprehend. Always, one of us looks away.

There are some moments when Patches reminds me of Friend. The way he throws his head back, and the sound of his laugh. When he doesn't let me get away without answering a question, and the shape of his shoulders when he walks, unconscious of the fact that I'm watching. I can't decide if I am actually warming up to Patches or if the similarities are just enough that I am tricking myself into thinking that I'm following Friend into the unknown.

But I know, the moments Patches breaks off into song or when he shyly looks away when I smile at him or when the light suddenly breaks off into darkness behind his eyes, I'm bonding with a real person again, not a memory or a ghost. It is hard for me. There is no room in my past experiences for new friends, just a small place to recognize new losses. I know very soon that I'm going to have to choose whether I let myself become attached to this man or whether I leave him.

I look around for something to distract me. I am surrounded by childhood treasures. A gilded box catches my eye. Because Patches is ahead of me, singing in another language which I now believe to be French, I give the box pause. Inside it is a Korean folded fan, a small ceramic doll with a painted face, a child's sheriff badge, and a portable CD player. I open the CD player and find that the compact disk inside it is plain black with no markings on it at all.

I take the CD and player, leaving the rest with the box, and catch up with Patches. I jog to his side and show him what I have found. He takes the CD out and turns it around, examining it thoroughly. Then replaces it and hands it back. If it were Friend, he would tell me that we don't have any speakers, and even if we did, we don't have any of the wires needed to hook them up. I would reassure him that I believed he could find a way. As it is someone else entirely, the response is closer to something I would say:

"It looks like we're about to have an adventure."

We spend the rest of the day picking through the Ruins until we find what we need to play the CD. I'm on amplification duty. I find a pair of speakers for a TV which does not help us at all, and I kick one over because I can, and let's face it, TV speakers are only useful with televisions, which are useless now. Nearby there is a little guitar amp against which sits a beautiful acoustic guitar with a slight pink tint to the wooden finish in near perfect condition. I grab them both and head back to our meeting place.

Patches is patrolling for the appropriate cords and batteries. He returns to our meeting spot with an armful of different wires and batteries spilling out, leaving a fairytale trail behind him. He unloads them all at my feet, abandoning this project at the sight of the wonderful musical instrument. Grabbing the guitar greedily, yet gently, he sits down at the first sturdy-looking spot he can find, and begins to tune it by ear.

I guess our adventure has quickly become *my* adventure. I set at it: plugging in wires and trying out batteries until I find the appropriate batteries for the amplifier and CD player and a wire to connect the two. I turn on the CD and adjust the volume.

A deep, dark voice fills the Ruins, overpowering Patches and the guitar. Suddenly the black CD makes perfect sense as a man who always wore black begins to sing. Patches takes only a moment before reproducing the chords of Johnny

Cash's first song on the guitar and begins singing along.

I smile at him and he drops a few lyrics to smile back at me. I set the CD player carefully on the amp and find a spot on an old blue chest to sit. Patches makes a great musician, and soon I cannot help but sing along as well, adding some harmonies to the mix. Our voices blend very well. Well, when we aren't taking turns impersonating Cash, that is.

There are exactly seventeen tracks on the CD. We play and sing through them all several times, then I turn off the CD and Patches plays a few well-known songs. I fashion a drum out of a garbage can, feeling a little like a hobo, but in a good way. After we exhaust his inventory of classics, he plays a few of the French songs. The drum doesn't go over too well, and we end up laughing about it, but the harmonies are a nice vocal touch, even if I do not know the lyrics.

We break for supper, and as I finish first, I claim the guitar for a while. I've only studied Classical guitar, so the mood shifts to a calmer, quieter tone. By the time I hand the guitar back to Patches, he takes to singing love songs and heartbreak songs and old folk ballads. I know about half of them. The songs I know we sing together or I take lead and Patches adds harmonies. The ones I do not know, he either teaches me or I add wordless vocalizations. At the end of it all, we are sitting side by side, playing the CD once more. Patches is improvising an alternate melody, and I'm leaning on Patches, drifting off.

"The songs you were singing earlier," I breathe sleepily as the last track finishes, "the French ones, who are they by?"

"Lori's brother, Jed, wrote them." Patches replies, lazily continuing to play. "He was a singer/songwriter who studied music in a private conservatory in France."

"Wow. Impressive."

"He was. I've never heard anyone as talented as Jed. I wish I were half the musician he was."

I look up at Patches. He doesn't return my gaze, but I think that may be ok just now.

"You're a wonderful musician, Patches. You just don't know it yet."

He stops playing. He might be giving me a funny look. I've closed my eyes, so I don't know.

"Is that a quote, Miracle?"

I yawn.

"No." I don't explain that it might be, it sounds familiar, but I don't remember. So I stand up and turn off the amp and the CD player.

"I'm exhausted," I explain to Patches' bemused expression. "Good night."

He watches his fingering as he mockingly plays me to my sleeping spot with Brahms Lullaby. I flip him off behind my back. He chuckles, but I'm asleep before I can really know how he responds.

The sun is rising over the Cascades. The blood-red fiery face beams up at the baby blue sky. There is one trail leading to the sun, and I am walking it alone. The sand underfoot is warm and pleasant. I abandon my shoes. I am wearing Patches' coat, but it is unraveling with each step that I take, until there is nothing left but a single thread dancing away like a spider's silk on the wind.

For a moment, I am my sister, her favorite purple and white sundress tickling the skin of my legs. I laugh, and it is a light, skipping, bouncing thing that echoes in the mountains. I shield my sister's eyes and look up at the sun, which has become white, like the flashing of a camera.

The sky is growing dark around the white sun, turning into a dark collage of colors that hail the deadliest of storms. Right before me, the clouds clump and twist together, stretching toward the sand. It expands into a great funnel, carrying darkness and the screech of death.

I cannot run. My sister's feet have sunken into the white sand, and buried, cannot be lifted. I watch the rise of the vortex, and then, I feel it pull my sister into it. First, the dress begins to flap against my sister, waving and whipping around her. Then, slowly, my sister is lifted up into the air, wafting towards the destructive storm.

And suddenly I am watching it all from a far off point. I see my sister rising into the air towards the storm, and I feel time, like sand, spinning in chaotic little circles around us all. I try to scream out her name, but all that comes out is a breath of shadow, and I find I cannot remember her name at all. Perhaps she has no name, perhaps it has simply been too long since I have uttered it, but I simply cannot force it out of my mouth.

When I try to call to her, there is a blinding flash as lightning from all around strikes my little sister. It lingers as she cries out like an illuminated cocoon in a spider's web. She is caught and the storm is fading. I run to the road, but by the time I get there, the funnel has melted away into the figure of a person dressed in brown and gray rags. The figure turns to me and its face is that of a wolf. When it locks onto my eyes with its own violet gaze, it curls its lips over its fangs and growls fiercely. It snaps its jaws at me and is gone, leaving a pool of water on the ground where it stood.

I run to the pool. It gleams silver up at me and holds only my reflection. I watch myself through the pool and I age before my eyes. I become old. My cheeks sag and my eyes hollow and there is a small, white worm that squirms out of my mouth and falls into the pool. The ripples cloud my vision until there are only unrecognizable plays of color and shadow in the water. Then, there is nothing.

When I wake, he is asleep, half-bent over, half-curled up in his namesake coat. Apparently he tried to fix it after I went to bed and fell asleep halfway through the project. The sewing kit is strewn across the ground at his feet. I gather it up for him and then take a good long look at him.

His lips are parted slightly and his whole body is relaxed. He is pale, although I am sure the same could be said about me. In this state, with his unmanageable, wonderful hair dancing down his neck and onto his back, and his small, but thick, dark facial hair, he looks like a lost knight in some enchanted sleep. Once again, as always, I wonder at the outcome of our venturing together.

I don't feel like dealing with this right now, so I take the rose guitar and find a quiet corner in which to play. The steel under my fingertips is familiar and reminiscent of a bygone age. I play through all my classical songs, and then close my eyes and play a few folk songs. My uncle was musically inclined, and he gave me the gift of a new song or two every family reunion.

We would find a quiet room, away from the bustle and commotion of old family recipes, and clashing football teams, and which parent of which distantly-related cousin might have pneumonia. Usually the most secluded rooms were bedrooms, so we would sit on whosever bed it was and take turns talking and playing music. He always taught me a folksong per my request, singing it in his slow, sweet tenor range until I could almost picture the notes of music, I knew them so well.

I let my muscle memory serve its purpose and the familiarity of the songs soothes me. Running the risk of waking Patches, I swallow once and let my voice remember how the songs feel rising out from my lungs to join the air. For a moment, my voice registers as my uncle's. I think he is here, but he's not, so I shut my eyes tighter and sing a little louder until I block out both past and present. All that exists is what lingers in the depth of my song.

Eighteen

I do not know how long I let myself escape this way. When my voice can no longer hold a note without breaking, I open my eyes. Reality is unforgiving as it regains its place around me. My fingers are raw and I've cut one almost to the point of bleeding from the amount of pressure I've applied to the strings of the guitar.

I lean the guitar against a pile of junk, whispering a prayer of thanks for the precious moments it gave me, and climb back through the ruins towards Patches. He is awake, working on his coat and rubbing his eyes free from their dreamy sand. He doesn't appear to have been up for very long, and there is still a lot of work left to patch up his coat.

I dig through my pack, looking for something to eat or something to do. I'm not hungry, however, and my pack is empty of everything except food, my father's camera, and my gun. I throw the bag aside, exasperated. Patches raises an eyebrow at me, but I have no answer for him except for a shrug and a sigh, so he goes back to his work. I start searching the ruins.

I find a lot of nothing. There is a stuffed dog with years of love and abuse worn into its matted fake fur. One eye is missing, but the other looks up at me as if it is still waiting for someone to come back and claim it. My heart aches to leave it be, without even holding it or helping it, but it would be impractical to lug a stuffed animal through the ruins, so it stays and I continue.

Eventually I come across a deck of cards. I open the moldy cardboard box that contains them. I have to go through the entire deck and peel apart every two or three cards. Some of them peel enough that their numbers are barely recognizable, but it doesn't matter much, they will still serve their purpose. Perhaps, I think bitterly, this will be the last time these cards will get to be used.

I sort the cards into their four suits and then arrange them in numerical order, checking to make sure none of the cards are lost. When I come to the Joker card, I set it aside. It will be my partner in crime for any games needing more than one player that I decide to play. First, though, I play solitaire. After I lose three games, win one, and lose two more, I decide to move on to a new game. So Joker and I play Garbage and then War. War, however, is a long and tedious game, so we decide- mutually of course- that we are bored with it and I put the cards back in their box. I decide I can afford to give up the space in my pack for a deck of cards, so I keep the deck.

On the way back to Patches, I find a book that doesn't appear to be too badly damaged. It is a romance novel, but those are fun sometimes. Besides, it isn't as if I have access to anything else, so I take it in case Patches is still working. He is. He is still bent over his coat, carefully stitching every patch back together with looping, uneven stitches.

"What did you find?" Patches asks, without glancing up at me.

"A deck of cards and a book." I reply.

"Yeah? What kind of book?"

"A smutty one." This merits a surprised look from the untalented seams-man. I smile. "It is called *Delicious Surrender*."

I hold up the book, flaunting its ridiculous cover. A woman with long, chocolate-colored hair and medieval clothes that barely cover her perfect body dances over a bed of grapes. She holds her skirt up ridiculously high and is looking off into the distance where the shadow of a man stands.

"Sienna, daughter of New Gloucester's master winemaker," I read from the back of the book. "has her hands full when her father dies right before the harvest, leaving the estate to an arrogant cousin from across the sea. Despite her misgivings

about her cousin, Byron, they are inexplicably drawn to one another in their passion for making remarkable wine." I stop and scrutinize.
"Sure...their passion for making... wine."

"Really?" Patches questions. "Aren't they cousins?"

"But! But... when Sienna uncovers a long kept secret regarding the bloodlines of the royal family, she discovers that sweet flavors sometimes come with a deadly aftertaste."

Patches drops his head and chuckles.

"I can't believe that is a real book." He says.

I sit down beside Patches and flip through a few pages of the book.

"What are you doing?"

I hold the majority of the book with my right hand, while my left thumb and index finger keep the cover and select pages from slapping shut.

"I'm playing find the climax. It's where you take turns flipping open to a random page in a smutty book and reading from that page until one person finds, well, the climax."

"Where did you learn that game?" He looks at me, eyebrows simultaneously pressed together and raised in quizzicality. I shrug.

"At a friend of mine's party. It was an all-girl thing so we did everything you could imagine in a stereotypical teenage girl sleepover. We watched bad romance movies and danced around to girly pop music and interrogated each other on who we liked. Then, when we were supposed to be sleeping, my friend produced this smutty book. She had inconspicuously picked it up at a truck stop during her last family vacation, and we passed it around, reading it by the light of flashlights in our sleeping bags. It was all very scandalous, really."

"Those types of things actually happen?"

"You know, they do. Not as often as most fantasies would hope, but they do."

He acknowledges the profound truth in my statement with a lifting of his eyebrows and a nod before he goes back to stitching. He's making an awful mess of it all. But he tries it with such determination and shows me his progress with such pride, that I don't dare intervene. I do, however, pick a piece of thread out of his curls.

I do not read *Delicious Surrender*, just look over the cover once more, laugh, and put it in my pack. Then I take out the cards and sit on the ground, shuffling them over and over again. It isn't much for entertainment, but I feel somehow comfortable just sitting here next to Patches, each of us engrossed in our own activities, yet enjoying each other's quiet company. At least, I enjoy his company. I have no way of knowing if he is happy here with me or not. I like to think he is. I like to think that, even if the world was still full of people, we would still choose moments like this.

"There!" He exclaims in time, pronouncing the completion of his repair. He throws on the coat and dances around for a few moments, making sure the range of movement is still there. "Perfect."

It is far from perfect. Just the weight of gravity is enough to pull at the large stitches. It is going to fall apart again very soon. However, the beaming joy on the face of my companion is enough to compel me to smile at him, and keep my comments and judgments regarding his craftsmanship to myself. When he turns back to me, catching my smile in his wide, uninhibited grin, I flash him the cards.

"Do you want to play a game or two?" I ask, feeling no need to set out again immediately.

"Sure. What games do you know?"

We pass a few names of card games we know back and forth, each not really knowing the games the other knows. Eventually, we decide on poker. After dealing the first hand, we recall we have nothing with which to bet. So we reach over and grab the first treasure from the Ruins that we can get. Patches produces a pair of sunglasses as his ante, and I slap a can opener into the pot.

We look at our cards, raise the pot until it contains our antes, an only slightly stained silk pillow, a pair of earrings, some shoelaces, and a pin in the shape and semblance of a cat. Patches was bluffing with a Queen high and I had a pair of tens, so I win and we reshuffle.

We play several hands, most of which I win because Patches has a tendency to bet every round regardless of his hand where I usually fold if I have nothing. So, while he gets several small antes, I usually claim the bigger pots. Although, he does get lucky a couple of times and wins with actually good hands.

After we play for a bit, we eat some lunch and pack up to go. One of our hands in Poker produces a necklace with a pendant of a swan, its head serenely folded back over her wings. I keep it, clipping it around my neck before we go. This time, when we fall silent on the road, it is a good silence filled with smiles and memories.

We stop early, before either of us is really weary, and I teach him to play Garbage. As the game goes on, we get sleepy. While we started sitting on the ground, we eventually lie down, propping ourselves up on out elbows. It takes longer and longer for us to take our turns, and while I am shuffling the deck, Patches falls asleep. I put the cards back in the box and let myself put my head

down on my scarf-made-pillow a few inches from
his.

He is strangely beautiful when he sleeps. His
skin seems softer and smoother, as if the calming of
his breathing has stilled every pore and feature. His
lips are slightly parted, though he still breathes from
his nose, and a single strand of hair rests
dangerously close to his lips. I hesitate a moment,
then brush it away. He furrows his brow ever so
slightly and turns away from me. I follow the spiral
of his curls with my eyes as I drift off to sleep.

*The world is nothing but darkness. I am in
terror, opening my eyes as wide as they can grow,
trying to find some form or light. There is nothing to
feed my vision. However, from somewhere nearby,
there is the rustle of paper. Paper?*

*"Friend?" I whisper very, very softly. "Are
you awake?"*

*"Did I wake you, Little Owl?" His voice is
low and reassuring.*

"No. What are you doing?"

"I couldn't sleep, so I was reading."

"Reading?"

*"Yes." I can hear the lightening of his voice
as he smiles. "With the goggles."*

"I didn't know we had any books."

"I just have the one. Tennyson."

"Tennyson?"

"Lord Alfred Tennyson, the poet. When I was in school, I had a professor who was just obsessed with Tennyson. In every class I had with him, he incorporated at least one of Tennyson's poems. "The Lotos-Eaters" and "Ulysses" for my Greek Legends class, "Lady of Shallot"- of course- and the "Idyls" for King Arthur- until I finally came up to him and asked if there were any courses he ever taught in which he did not mention Tennyson.

'Not one.' He told me. 'For Tennyson and Folklore are intricately entwined. Poets are the reason folktales still exist and Tennyson is one of the finest.'

"On the day of my graduation, that same professor gave me a pocketbook of Tennyson's works. I've kept it on my person at all times."

"Oh." I return. "Will you read aloud? I don't know that I've ever heard his poetry."

"Of course, Little Owl.

'Tis strange that those we lean on most,
Those in whose laps our limbs are nursed,
Fall into shadow, soonest lost:
Those we love first are taken first.

God gives us love. Something to love
He lends us; but, when love is grown

To ripeness, that on which it throve
Falls off, and love is left alone.

    This is the curse of time. Alas!
In grief I am not at all unlearn'd;
Once thro' mine own doors Death did pass;
One went, who never hath return'd.

    He will not smile- not speak to me
Once more. Two years his chair is seen
Empty before us. That was he
Without whose life I had not been.

    Your loss is rarer; for this star
Rose with you thro' a little arc
Of heaven, not having wander'd far
Shot on the sudden into dark.

    I knew your brother: his mute dust
I honour and his living worth:
A man more pure and bold and just
Was never born into the earth.

    I have not look'd upon you nigh,
Since that dear soul hath fall'n asleep.
Great Nature is more wise than I:
I will not tell you not to weep.

    And tho' mine own eyes fill with dew,
Drawn from the spirit thro' the brain,
I will not even preach to you,
  "Weep, weeping dulls the inward pain."

> *Let Grief be her own mistress still.*
> *She loveth her own anguish deep*
> *More than much pleasure. Let her will*
> *Be done- to weep or not to weep."*

I close my eyes. What sad words, yet comforting, to be spoken in this place. I like the idea that no one should say to someone whether or not to weep, because grief affects each heart differently. I drift away from the darkness on the echo of the last verse I can hear.

> *Let Grief be her own mistress still.*
> *She loveth her own anguish deep*
> *More than much pleasure. Let her will*
> *Be done- to weep or not to weep.*

Let her will be done- to weep or not to weep.

I wake to realize we've both moved in our sleep. We are huddled close to each other, each on our side, facing one another. Patches has one arm lazily around me and my face is tucked down near his chest. It is very warm and wonderful. I can feel his breath tickling the back of my neck. If time really were to stop, I would wish it to be in this moment.

Suddenly, in a harsh moment, it occurs to me that I do not trust this man and I should not be here. My eyes open in actual waking, and I can feel the pounding of my heart throughout my entire body. I wonder, fleetingly, if he can feel it too. I think about what I should do. If I move, he will wake. If I stay, he will wake. I take a breath, and pretending to sleep, roll over so my back is to him.

There is a change in his breathing for only one sigh, than he settles. I inch away slowly, until it is just his fingertips draped on my waist. I turn ever so slightly so that his fingers slide down onto the ground without falling. I inch away a little bit then stop, faking sleeping for a few moments in case he should wake. He doesn't. I stand, shivering at the sudden change of temperature.

I rub at my eyes. Why do I feel even more tired than when I fell asleep? I feel as if I had no sleep at all. Perhaps that had something to do with moving around enough to reach Patches and the drop of the temperature. Oh well. I drink some water to try and clear my foggy head. After a few sips, I look up and the sight startles me enough to drop the water. It spills and runs away from me and the Thunderbourne that is staring me in the face.

Nineteen

I am still holding my pack over one shoulder. I thrust my hand into the pack and draw forth my gun, cock it, and fire as quickly as I can at the demon's head. The sound of the shot brings Patches to his feet quicker than he can snap out of sleep. He staggers a few steps back, trying to make sense of the scene.

Once he recognizes the danger, he is very quick to draw and wield his butterflies. Cutting through the air with an almost inhuman speed, Patches jumps between the creature and me. He holds a defensive position. I ready the gun and point it at the creature over Patches' shoulder, my arm extended and my hand steady. The creature locks eyes with Patches, and then disappears. Patches closes his knives and spins around to me. I drop my arm to my side.

"Are you ok?" Patches tries desperately to catch my eyes, but they stay downcast, looking at the gun.

"Hey." He tries again, ducking slightly to the side to catch my gaze, holding it as he straightens. "Are you alright? Did it hurt you?"

I shake my head, unable to find my voice. He throws his arms around me, embracing me. I rest my head on his shoulder. I can feel his heart, his warmth. I return his embrace with the one arm that is not holding a weapon.

There is, without warning, a great and terrible flash of green light somewhere in the heart of the Ruins. It lasts only a few blinding seconds, but it is enough to lurch my heart and elicit a terrified moan from my lips. A moment later, the thunder-cap follows, leaving my ears ringing. The lightning has left the hair on the back of my neck and arms raised. I look into the wide, searching eyes of Patches and pull away from him.

"The Gathering?" I exhale.

He nods, his face grim.

"What will you do?" I already know the answer before I ask the question. It is written all over him: the way he stands, the way he breathes, the way his eyes harden and set on a certain point on the horizon. He turns and puts a hand on my shoulder. His touch burns into my soul and I twist away.

"I have to go back." I can feel the tears well. "I have to see what has happened. You have to keep going. It isn't safe for you here, and I'm not allowed to bring you to the community."

I know if I try to argue I will lose composure, so I give him a very pained look and nod. He returns the look wrapped in a fleeting smile.

"Good. Keep going in the direction we were headed. You should reach the end of the Ruins very soon. I will meet you in the heart of Strongwood, if not sooner. Keep going, Miracle, and don't look back."

We embrace one more time. I want to hold on to him forever. I wish I could clutch his hair. I wish I could wrap his warmth around me forever. I wish I could kiss him. I let go. I just watch him take the endless steps away from me, and when he is gone, I bury my gun.

I replace grandfather's knife in its proper place and walk briskly away from our parting ground. Only three tears escape, and I swat them off my cheeks before they can leave their imprint on my skin. To hell with what Tennyson wrote, I will not let Grief be master of me today. Today, I will not weep. Today, I will survive.

Patches was right about the edge being close. I reach it after only two more wake-spans of walking through the Ruins. I keep a vigorous pace, not really considering what I break as I step on a lifetime of belongings, each with their own perishable stories. I also throw out the book and scatter the cards to the wind as if they were the ashes of some dead loved one. I make sure the Joker is the last card I part with, and I give him a kiss goodbye for everyone I could not send off properly.

I do not think their names. I do not recall their faces. I push past it all, locking it up in a secluded part of my heart. I imagine it an island surrounded by mist. I imagine I row away from the island. Someday, I will go back, but now I can only go forward.

When I sleep, I dream of demons. As much as I can, I let them fade away from me with the breaking of the sleep-span. I do not try to recall them and I no longer wonder who it is that I am supposed to be saving. There are no souls to follow me anymore. I am really alone now, and it is almost peaceful living in utter apathy.

The edge of the Ruins is more like a slow, vanishing point. The woods are taller than I recall trees being. Then again, everything up until this point has been close and low to the ground. The way they stand so proudly gives me strength. Not only did they survive the wind, the magnificent trees have not even bowed a little when it howled.

I run my hand over the hard, scaly bark of a nearby tree. The beginning of the forest is littered with a few items that crossed the threshold by wind or will. I linger at this new landscape, gathering a few more supplies of food and drink. I find some more canned goods, a bag of dry cereal, a box of probably stale crackers, and some water. I also find two cans of diet soda. I never really liked the flavor of artificial sweeteners, but I take them anyway because it is a treat.

The litter of the Ruins fades away into the soft, damp cushion of leaves and underbrush. Where I had to watch to avoid stepping on man-made obstacles in the Ruins, now I watch so I do not trip on rocks or fallen branches. The tall, fully leafed trees block out most of the sky and almost all of the hidden, stagnant sun. There are, however, tiny burnt-orange lights that flicker throughout the forest, like the brightest of fireflies or some sort of faerie creature. The lights illuminate the forest well enough for me to see, but they always disappear before I can catch up to see their source.

There is no wind in the woods, although the air tastes fresh and warm. I remove my jacket and tie it around my waist. My scarf goes into my pack. I even remove my shoes, for a while, and walk barefoot. There is a calm to the forest that slows my steps and memories. Not enough to be sinister, of course, this is not a land of lotuses. It is nice to be leisurely.

I come across a pool underneath the shadow of a tree whose roots circle around it, looking like ornate knot-work. The water is clear and cool. I slip off my pack and my clothes and bathe in the pool. If any spirit or creature of the forest minds my presence in the pool, there is no indication. I lean back and rinse out my hair, massaging the scalp with my fingertips.

I let myself soak, basking in the pumpkin-and-spice colored lights and the tranquility until my fingers wrinkle. I am relaxed enough that I may just fall asleep at any moment. I climb out and spread my clothes out over a pile of leaves. That is where I will make my nest for this sleep-span. It is balmy enough that I do not even feel chilled as I sleep wet and naked, on the forest floor.

There are no dreams, just deep, uninterrupted, beautiful sleep.

When I blink my eyes open, the fact that I am dried off is the only evidence that time has passed. I stretch out my arm, feeling the welcoming leaves, breathing in the smell of moist earth all around me. I sit up, stretching some more, then stand. One by one, I pick up each article of clothing, shake or brush the dirt off, wash it in the pool, and hang it on a nearby branch to dry. I eat some breakfast as I wait.

The clothes do not dry well because the air is so close and there is no wind, but it is warm enough that the moisture in the fibers does not bother me much. I wear my underwear, bra, wrap pants and tank top. I manage to rearrange my pack to stuff my leggings and jacket in it. I roll up my socks and put them in my boots, which I carry. I know this means that my feet will become dirtier much quicker, but the boots are hot and clunky, and I love the feel of the soft earth under my heels.

I do not really know where I am going, but I go on anyway. I actually have no idea how I will ever know when- or if- I reach the center of the forest. For all I know, I could already be in the heart of Strongwood. I doubt it, though. I think such an old and mythical forest as this would be larger than that.

All of the trees here are different from each other. Each has a unique texture and design to its bark, special shades of green for their leaves, and an inimitable shape, reach, or form. Some have asymmetrical leaves, some have branches that seem to grow downward rather than upward, and quite a few have white, peeling bark instead of thick, brown bark.

I take my time traveling through Strongwood. I linger to admire certain trees. I trail my hands on the smooth, spiky, or bumpy bark. I climb trees, if their form allows it, laughing at the sap that covers my hands. I chase the lights. I dance to my own songs, and no songs at all.

I live for many wake-spans like this. I find many pools to wash in and enjoy. I sleep naked on soft leaves and I never dream. When I wake, I feel rested. When I am tired, I fall asleep right away. Nothing is difficult in this magical place.

When I wake, the little lights are all hovering near me, casting the forest into the look and feel of a perpetual twilight. I feel a slight ringing in my head as if it contains a beautiful song that has slipped just past memory but lingers in my heart's recognition. I think the forest is trying to speak to me, and if so, the language is beautiful and the message is kind.

I still cannot get very close to the lights, they duck out of the way and show up elsewhere, but they let me get tantalizingly near them first. The lights are mischievous as well. They seem to be attracted to my swan necklace, which is always around my neck, even when I sleep. They jump in front of me so they can catch their reflection in the shining metal wings. When they do this, they blind me for a moment, and then skitter away. I imagine they laugh to themselves as they flee.

Sometimes they do this when I sleep. That is when it is the most annoying. I'm not used to bright flashes being playful, but harmless things. I always jump awake, screaming, and they scatter. But nothing in Strongwood has ever frightened or threatened me, so my head knows that I shouldn't be afraid here, and that makes this place my favorite in the whole wide world.

If only Patches were here, it'd be like our own Eden. Except, he'd probably never stay here as long as the Gathering exists. He did come with me this far, but I'm sure it wouldn't last if actually tested. I wonder if Friend would have followed me here. Would he have stayed here with me? He stayed with me in despair, would he have stayed with me in hope?

I go to the nearest tree. She stands beautifully tall and elegant, with a thin trunk covered in smooth, white and silver bark, stretching her slight branches up and away from her body as if she had just woken up and were stretching. Her leaves are small and silvery-green. Maybe she liked the color of frost enough that, even after spring arrived, she kept it about her. I put my right hand gently on her trunk and press my forehead and nose against her bark in greeting.

"You are beautiful." I whisper to her, although I'm sure she already knows. The lights spin around her trunk, dancing through her branches. I let my hand trail across her as I step away.

When I move away, the lights follow me. I turn and they scatter, hiding behind trees and in piles of leaves. I walk a bit slower, knowing they are behind me, then I turn quickly, as if they were children and I was trying to make them jump. They follow in the same manner while I dance, jump, climb, and run. Each time I play with the suspension of knowing they are behind me and laughing when they try and hide.

However, when I hide behind a tree, then jump out to play with the lights, I find them unusually still and dispersed among the forest. One little light is hovering near the ground at the foot of a large, sturdy, rust-colored tree not so far from me. To my shock, the light shudders and disappears into the shadow of the forest. As it does so, there is a sighing sound that ripples from the rusty tree, as if it is exclaiming a sad "oh."

Another light, lingering underneath a skeleton leaf on the forest floor, flickers away like a candle flame being blown out. Again, there is a high-pitched exhale from a tree. I cannot place the tree who sighs this time. The skeleton leaf, who sheltered the poor, disappearing light, shrivels and dies, curling up on itself until it distorts into a mummified cocoon.

Two more lights, spinning around each other nervously, disappear. Another follows and another, until the whole forest is filled with the weeping and wilting of trees, crying out for the playful lights that have all gone out. Only a small handful of the lights remain, clumped together and shakily glowing their cinnamon luminescence as brightly and courageously as they can.

If the forest was calm when content, it is utterly restless now, as if every particle of life in Strongwood has awakened. I can breathe the sorrow born here. I can feel it enter into me, and I know I am a part of the forest. Without the conscious decision to do so, I begin to mimic the sounds of Strongwood's grief. No tears fall, but my breath rises and falls with the spirit of the trees, and every time a light falls, I die inside.

I spin around to locate any other precious luminaries still living and find none left at all. Instead, small slits of pale green begin to appear in pairs. All of Strongwood shudders at the revelation. Many trees droop and shed tear-covered leaves. Several scream out into the air, piercing my heart and my courage to the very core.

Twenty

Thunderbourne. Of course. These damned creatures followed me from the depths of shadows through the tunnels of the dead, and I let them all out when I surfaced. I opened a door that I could not close and did not think about the repercussions of my actions. They never stopped hunting. I have been leading them to newer prey, more ripe with life than they ever could have found in the Underground.

I was clever enough to find the way out of Skeleton and through the Storm Lands, around the swamp and to the Ruins. I followed Patches close enough to the Gathering so I'm sure the horrors found them easily. Then, he and I were so good as to show them through the maze of the Ruins and invite them over the threshold into Strongwood.

They must hunger for, or lust after, destruction. They consume life wherever they come across it. And they have let me live because that would be the advantageous thing to do; because I have a tendency to lead the Thunderbourne to their prey. I have been finding life everywhere I go. I am paying for my survival with the deaths of everyone

I encounter. I think back to the old woman in Underground and her prophecy.

"You are a woman with the strength to survive all of this, but if you do survive, you will be alone. The last of the living in this land."

I had thought her prophecy only true in Underground. It appears that is not the case. Was it even a prophecy, or was it a warning? If I had left her when she had spoken these words, if I hadn't had let Sights pull me back up to the platform, if I had held my breath and pretended I wasn't there, would they still be alive? Would I?

I do not know what to do. The lights are gone, the people are gone, the trees are in mortal danger, and I am afraid. With shaking hands, I pull on my boots. I do not bother with the socks; they stay as they were, bunched up at the toes of my inherited footwear. The laces I quickly, and sloppily, knot and stuff into the boots so they do not accidentally trip me. Then, I run.

I do not know where I am going, only that I must lead the Thunderbourne away from my friends. I do not stop to make sure my lure is working. I just run, letting the cold, gray light from somewhere far above me light my way. I stumble and fall quite a few times. It takes more and more effort to continue. Eventually, I fall and stay down.

It starts in my childhood bedroom. I am young and curled up in the wooden bed I've had since my sister was born. The bed is directly underneath a window covered by sheer, pink and purple curtains. Ah, yes. That is what those colors look like. My best and most beloved stuffed animals and toys litter the room. This was where I was always the most comfortable. This was where my mother would sing me to sleep. This is where the angels would comfort me when the demons found me.

There is an eerie green glow accumulating right outside my window, peering into the room to the march of a distant rumbling. The noise and light tease my mind until it lingers close to waking. This is where the demons like me- too far wrapped in the grip of sleep to resist, yet conscious enough to recognize and remember everything that will happen.

It is a world of its own, full of shade and panic. I squirm against the light, the rumbling, the faraway wind, and the way my body reacts to it all. Nothing exists but the panic and the glow. The rest of the world fades into darkness, melting away from the window which remains open to let cool night air into the warm room.

This window will be my downfall, as it is open, allowing access.

I stumble to my knees, no longer a child. The sheet hovers a moment against my bare skin, then falls to my lap. I am illuminated, pale skin in unearthly glow. I reach under the curtains, too afraid to look at what could be outside. With force, and quivering hands, I slam the window shut, and exhausted beyond belief from fighting sleep for so long, I fall to my back on the bed.

I breathe, letting my control slip away. It feels good to let go of my will. Too late, I realize the demons may have already gotten through the window before I shut it. This time, the panic surrounds me. I turn, defensive, to my room, and the glow touches my back, like eyes.

Beads of sweat tingle as they formulate on my brow. I turn again, but the eyes linger where I cannot see them: behind me. I lay on my back, remembering my days as a child when I realized that the demons could stab me through the bed as well. Nothing would protect me. By now, I am beyond exhausted. I am desperately clinging to my will, but as I lose the fight, it slips away.

I move. I am running barefoot out of my house. I am on the crest of a snow-covered mountain, though the cold does not register on my feet. A pack of wolves the color of shadows follows behind me. They howl and gnash their fangs against

*the air, lips curled around white teeth splattered
with crimson.*

*They snap at my heels and I go down. I
scream as I fall. They eat my flesh, tearing it, bit by
bit off my bones, starting at my feet and working
their way up to my hips, my shoulders, my neck, and
my face. The more they devour, the closer I come to
waking. They eat my eyes before I wake and the
world goes dark.*

I force my eyes to open and find that I am
sitting in a tall, mossy green tree, with no
recollection of having climbed it. The tree is higher
than many of the other trees in the forest, with me
near the top. I am overlooking the forest, which
seems endless and old. It is very windy here, cold
even. My coat is somewhere below. My shoulders
are bare and I have no way to cover myself.

There is a rustle above me. I look up and see
the silhouette of a figure I know all too well. *Friend
finds me, sitting over the forest with nothing
between me and the sky except the thoughts which
weigh me down.* My eyes are weary from the silvery
light of the sun through clouds and I am sure they
reflect the apathy of one who has shed more tears
than I thought I had inside me. I look away, back to
the comfort of the forest. If he said even one word,
it would break me.

Friend is wearing his gray pajama pants, a dark blue sweatshirt over a dark colored tee-shirt, and his own set of army boots. Through my peripheral vision, I see him run a hand through his dark brown hair which is just long enough to start to curl. He is beautiful, and more so, he is gentle. He found a home in my heart long ago, so all the walls I've built up are in vain.

"What are you doing, Little Owl?" he whispers, shattering me completely. I turn to look at him, wanting desperately to touch him. He is so very real. He is so very alive. He has followed me through the shadows of life and chased me here. He is so very beautiful. I swallow.

"Once, long ago," *I respond, fighting the urge to close my eyes or touch his face.* "I thought I was part of a love story. But I was so very young and it wasn't real. It was only an elaborate fantasy I indulged in for a time."

Friend lowers himself to my branch and sits behind me, wrapping his arms around me. He is trying to prove he is real. I can feel his breath on my neck.

"I promise you," I gasp to the forest, then turn to look into his eyes for the last time. "I will not make that mistake again."

The world freezes. His face stills in an expression somewhere between hurt and compassion. I want neither from him, and I know I will give him both before the end. Only, the end has already come. This man is gone and I will never see him again. This is the last time I will be able to touch him.

I lean my head on his chest, convincing myself that I can still feel his warmth, his breath; I can reach behind me and run my fingers through his hair at the base of his neck; I can smell the campfire smell that I always equate with him; I can keep him. I never have to wake up. As soon as I think that, I do.

Twenty-One

Nothing is the same after that. The forest is frightened. I climb down and stumble on through the world cast in light so gray that nothing seems real. The trees seem ominous. The underbrush is a snare, manageable only by slight movements that are impossible to accomplish in my boots.

I run out of supplies. I've eaten every can of food, finished every bottle of water, and both cans of soda. There is a small tree that has been trampled by something. It bends horribly to one side, though it is not broken, so I leave my coat at its base to prop it up. I am sure the Thunderbourne will render my attempts to preserve life useless by devouring the young, vulnerable thing as soon as I step away, but I must not let myself give in to that despair.

I must continue like I was something good. I have to make myself worthy of being alive. If it is true, that the only reason I survive is because I've sacrificed countless lives to the Thunderbourne, then I must carry that responsibility with me. I have to be better for the world than all of their lives combined.

Up ahead of me there is the impossible, yet unmistakable, flickering of a light. This isn't one of the living lights, its almost-blue tint gives away that it is inanimate. I pause mid-step, leaving my left leg extended in the air right before touching the ground. I am unbalanced, but I will myself to keep steady. If I listen very closely, I can hear voices.

I crouch down and approach as quietly as I can, ducking behind the trees. I hope they have forgiven me at least enough that they would protect me if my life were in danger… not that I could protect them when their lives were, well, are in trouble. I shake my head of this thought and continue until I come to the center of the orb of light and can see what is happening without being seen.

The light is a flashlight, flickering in the distance because its bearer is waving it wildly about as he gesticulates angrily. It is Patches. Despite this recognition, I stay hidden. The transformation of the man before me, not in looks, but in behavior compels me to shrink away. He is angry. Much more angry than I've ever seen him and the one to whom his anger is aimed is there as well.

It is a girl. She looks to be in her mid-teens with long, golden hair contained in a braid over one shoulder. She stands very still, her slight build trembling only slightly despite the wild ravings of a man almost twice her height and build. She takes Patches in with steady, emerald eyes outlined in smeared, smoky makeup. She wears a short sundress that fits her perfectly. I am in awe of her beauty.

Her arms are held behind her, as if bound. I don't want to think that Patches would ever be capable of binding someone and maybe even taking them prisoner, yet I would in a heartbeat if I needed to. I cannot see to either confirm or disprove the theory that she is bound. She stands directly in front of me, so I cannot look behind her at all. In fact, if she were to look out at the forest, instead of keeping such a focused gaze on Patches, the girl would most likely see me.

Patches flies everywhere around the girl, not saying anything, but saying everything with his eyes. Disapproval. Disappointment. Desperation. He is perfectly terrifying this way, like some monster has possessed him putting that flame behind his eyes. He trips on the corner of his coat, and practically tears it off himself and slams it at the ground.

The girl's bare shoulders begin to tremble. Patches catches the movement and pounces like a high-strung cat. He grabs her, pulling her to turn to him, and she gasps. The response brings him back a little from whatever dark place he has existed within. He touches his forehead to her and whispers something to her, closing his eyes.

"It is my decision, sweetheart." She says in a breathy, shaking voice, closing her eyes in a slight relaxation. He pulls away slightly.

"You are not alone." He insists.

She smiles, but does not open her eyes. He brings her close to him and kisses her. Once, a small, quick peck on the lips. Twice, a lingering sigh of a kiss. Thrice, with longing to which she responds. The fourth time their lips meet, it is so Patches can whisper something into the far right corner, the corner reserved for secrets, of her mouth.

She furrows her brow in pain, then pulls away, shaking her head. Patches tugs at her braid with his left hand, tracing the outline of her jaw with his right. She squirms a little, trying to free herself from his touch. He wraps his arms around her, embracing her with everything he has. Every muscle in her body relaxes for a moment. She lifts her head, looking to the sky, biting her lower lip. Then she draws herself up and steps back.

"Please." Patches pleads, reluctantly releasing her.

She smiles at him through streaming, silent tears, and flashing him chattering, white teeth.

"I can't do it." She laughs, sadly. "I can't stand against these creatures. I don't know any tricks or possess any survival skills. I'm useless to you. I'd only hold you back; I'd just get you killed and I could never forgive myself that. It's better this way."

"You're not useless, Cara, and I don't care if you hold me back. You could bring the whole army of those demons on us, and I would rather it end that way than this way."

She blinks, her smile melting away into an impassable determination.

"Don't you see?" She tries to explain, "I don't want to live through this."

The girl moves her right arm, bringing a pistol to her own temple. Patches eyes go wide. I'm sure mine do too. She wasn't bound, but maybe she should have been. She cocks the gun. I want him to move, to wrestle the gun away from the girl, something! But he does not. He stares at her, darkly, as she takes a final, sobbing breath and pulls the trigger.

Patches stands there for a great, long time, pale as moonlight and just as isolated. Then, slowly, painstakingly, he begins to pick up every piece he can find of the girl's shattered skull. He kneels down to her and tries to put her back together. His fingers shake too much and he looks at them, bewildered, not knowing why he holds the pieces of a girl.

I bury my head in the trunk of my hiding place, sinking down to my knees. I can hear my friend crying. Each tear sounds like it would shatter a rib or two with its force and anguish. I press my fists against my ears. This is what I've brought into the world. This is what my survival has wrought. I curl into myself and weep like I've never wept before. All I know is that shot will always echo in the deepest part of me.

My sobs end before his. When I steady myself enough to look again, he is cradling her, rocking back and forth, singing one of his French love songs as if he's singing her to sleep. Maybe he is. He is seeped in Cara's blood and brains and sunshine-colored hair. His coat, on the ground next to him, is ruined.

Futilely, I recall my grandmother teaching me that if I ever needed to get a blood stain out of an article of clothing, I could use saliva. It would have to be saliva from the same person whose blood I wanted removed. Saliva has properties that naturally clean one's own blood. It is why so many animals lick their wounds and children naturally know to suck on their finger if cut. Not that any of Cara's saliva remains. Even if it did, it would take a lake and a hundred years to wash the coat free.

Patches seems to have the same thought because he takes his eyes off Cara and looks despondently at his favorite belonging. He takes the gun from the girl's fingers and throws it aside. He hesitates, then lifts the same hand and presses it against his lips. He can barely pucker his lips because they want to stretch and pull down with each breathless sob. He kisses her hand, and then holds it to his forehead as he weeps endlessly.

I put my back to the trunk of the tree and hug my knees to my chin. I make myself as small as I can be, as small as I feel inside. It isn't enough. I didn't know this girl, this Cara, so why am I so affected? Is it because Patches so clearly loved her? Is it because I love Patches and am jealous that he loves another? Is it because I feel guilty for releasing the Thunderbourne? Is it because I never got to share last words with my loved- and lost-ones?

I peak around the trunk. Patches is spreading his coat over Cara like the hospital people used to spread white sheets over the dead. He tucks her in, cocooning her into the folds of fabric like he slept in it.

In the middle of the sleep-span, I am crying. I cry silently, trying not to wake Friend, who lies near enough that I can hear his breathing. I try to match it. If I could hear his heartbeat, I think I would try to match it. My breaths remain broken, my heartbeat racing, no matter how I try to calm myself. All that results is that I end up hiccupping.

Friend takes a deep breath and groans a little. He is waking up. I freeze, holding my breath even though I know that it is a dead giveaway for someone pretending to sleep. However, if he does not wake fully, my breathlessness will ensure that I do not accidentally wake him. I hope he falls back asleep soon, as I can feel a hiccup building. It escapes.

"Little Owl?" Friend slurs sleepily, "Are you alright?"

"Yes." I sob.

He scoots closer to me. I can feel his warmth.

"You don't have to hide. You have nothing to be ashamed of. Least of all tears."

I can't stop crying, hiccupping, sobbing. I try to talk, to tell him how strong I want to be. They all catch in my throat. So he speaks instead, wiping at my eyes with his thumb and tucking a blanket under my chin.

"You know, some people don't expect perfection."

"That's a relief." I manage through the intake of uneven breaths.

Friend laughs. I will never forget the sound of that laugh. Or the way his lips felt as they brushed my forehead that night.

I will never forget the way it was to be able to share anything with him and be closer to him for it, instead of driven away. I wish someone could hear me cry now. I wish someone cared. More than anything, I wish I could have Friend back. Since I do not know who I am alone, I close my eyes and mourn in the way the trees of Strongwood have taught me: tearless and sighing.

Twenty-Two

Eventually, the shudders stop. Strongwood is still. The memory of blood stains and smell have faded slightly since Cara was shot three sleep-spans ago, and we've set off.

Patches found me, eventually. I looked out, he looked at me, and there were no words we could say to each other. So he came to me and offered his hand. I took it and stood up. I longed to embrace him. I wanted to comfort him and I wanted him to comfort me. However, since he could no more turn into Friend as I could turn into Cara, I locked away some important part of me, and we moved out.

Patches has supplies, but neither of us have much of an appetite, so we drink the water, and sometimes, the juice from canned fruit. Everything is flavorless. Words are flavorless and dry on my lips. I do not think I've spoken since our reunion except, apparently, during my sleep.

I've been sleeping fitfully, caught in the place where I cannot remember my nightmares beyond the cold sweat they leave me with. Patches doesn't sleep at all. He walks around; I never know if he will be there when I wake. He is always awake, wandering. When I fall asleep, he is always awake, wandering. When I wake, the same.

I don't know where we are going. Yet, it seems, I'm destined to lead. Patches follows me, watching me with affected, empty eyes. He is the absolute reflection of the Thunderbourne that followed me for so long. He lingers, and when I look at him, all I see are his terrifying eyes, that are always devoid of every passion, every inclination of soul.

I know, eventually, he will get better. He has to. Right now, however, it is very hard to see myself this way, much less someone else. I don't even know if he sees me well enough to notice that I'm as heartbroken as he is. Maybe I'm too good at hiding. After all, I am a master of deception, guarded by years of darkness and jaded by loss. Or, maybe, he's not very good at seeing through the darkness. Maybe he can't hear the silence.

So. I guess I'm alone again. Maybe, if I think of him as just another ghost following me around to haunt me, it will hurt me less that he refuses to acknowledge me. I want to slap him. I want to snap him out of this fog so we can get through this together because I cannot get through this alone. Not this time.

I stop. Patches runs into me. I mutter an apology, and continue walking. There's a black pit that has just consumed my stomach and heart and is now squeezing my lungs, trying to get them as well. The old woman's words circle around my head, replaying and echoing into eternity. That prophecy, or warning, or curse, or whatever it is, will never leave me alone until it is ultimately fulfilled.

Unconsciously, I dwell on Cara's last words. Do I want to live in this world anymore? Once, so long ago, I wanted this. I did not care if I would be alone, I wanted to be alive. I was willing to leave a group of people I cared about- a family- for the chance that I could live. I never thought "how could we all live?" or even "I want us to live." No, I had to just think of me. I wanted to survive. I. Me. Maybe I deserve to be alone; it would serve me right for all of my selfish decisions. However, no one deserved to die for me.

I cannot help it, I begin to cry. I thought all my tears would be dry by now, but they continue to amaze me with their fresh supply. I force myself to go through the list. I do not count my family, because I cannot prove that I was the cause of their deaths. Friend. I can't prove I was responsible for his death, but he stayed for me. Perhaps he could have survived if he hadn't stayed, if he hadn't found me, or if he had overcome his good heart and just left me at the tree to cry forever.

The group from the Underground. It's been so long that I do not even remember all of their names. I accuse myself at that fact. If I ever needed proof that I was too selfish to deserve such a family, there it is. I try to prove myself wrong: Sights, who was blind and always watched over me; the old woman, who led the expedition and caught the future in her dreadlocks; Red, the one who walked between despair and disappearance... I can't do this. Their names all come flooding back, but I hate it.

Patches was right, they were names. People can't go without names. This naming system was just rigged to make sure actions were taken to personal, individual advantage. I never really cared who they were; all I cared about was who they were to me, which turns out, was a sacrificial slaughter for my gain.

I am so angry at myself. I grit my teeth and I'm moving faster than before. Patches does not seem to notice any of this, not my crying, not my speed, not the inevitable doom to which I am leading him. Oh well. If he is to die, at least they will take this shell, this husk of the beautiful man I once knew instead of the real him. *Too bad, Thunderbourne, someone already took the real him away.*

I sniff the tears away and glance back at husk-man. I am taken aback by how utterly worn out he appears. I stop, so he does as well. I suggest that he try to sleep. He gives me a brief, glazed glance. *I know, Mr. Insomniac, but you have to sleep sometime.*

"Look," I say, hoping he's at least listening a little. "I've fallen asleep first the past three sleep-spans. It is your turn. I'm not falling asleep until you do."

He looks at me. Well, that's new. He doesn't turn away for a while. When he does, he lies down on the ground. He's not actually asleep. Any fool could see that, and I was trained to notice even the subtle details of fake sleeping. Sights was no fool. I suppose I should be grateful that he even listened to me at all.

After he is still for a while, with no sign of getting up to wander, I think about sleeping. However, Patches still needs sleep, and he isn't going to if I pass out now. He will just get up and pretend like I never saw a thing. I do the only thing I can think of to make sure he stays where he has feigned sleep; I lie down next to him.

He stiffens dramatically. This isn't surprising; I'm actually relieved. *That's right. Acknowledge that I'm here.* I snuggle closer to him and even am so bold as to put an arm around him.

Then I slow my breathing and let him think I have fallen asleep. He stays put. He doesn't respond to me, or relax, or sleep, but he also doesn't get up to wander restlessly so I think I've won this battle.

As I drift off, I find myself letting Patches comfort me. I like his radiant warmth, even when it is as warm as it is in this forest. I like pressing my nose into his soft curls, which I still don't know how he keeps clean, but are by no means greasy or dirty. I like that he is here, whether or not I deserve him.

There is a woman, weeping for a man as they so often do, and I am a tear upon her cheek. I try to caress her, to comfort her, but she swats me away and I end up on her finger. This place is colder than the warmth of her face. I'm chilled as her finger moves and the cold, stark wind hits me.

The finger alights upon a page, an old page, one I hesitate to sit upon. Searching for warmth, I land. The woman curses herself and tries to wipe me away from her precious book. However, I am already in, soaked into the fibers of the page, resting my head in their margins. I wonder how I ever lived in an eye, in a sad woman, when I could have lived here, where the only sorrow is in interpretation.

The lady's eye was not untrained, so I read the words with ease:

"In this poor gown my dear lord found me first,
And loved me serving in my father's hall:
In this poor gown I rode with him to court,
And there the Queen array'd me like the sun;
In this poor gown he bade me clothe myself,
When now we rode upon this fatal quest
Of honour, where no honour can be gain'd:
And this poor gown I will not cast aside
Until himself arise a living man,
And bid me cast it, I have griefs enough:
Pray you be gentle, pray you let me be:
I never loved, could never love but him:
Yea, God, I pray you of your gentleness,
He being as he is, let me be."

*And where I read the words, there they
vanish, dead at my touch like crumbling cities of
gold.*

When I wake, my right hand is completely numb. Patches and I are sprawled away from each other, but are holding onto each other's hand. I squeeze it tightly, as I look around us and realize that we are completely surrounded by approaching Thunderbourne.

They rise, like someone's shadow rose up from the ground to discover all the dimensions of reality. Looking at them is as staring into nothingness. I let go of Patches' hand, gently placing it on his chest. He does not wake, not even when I stand and address the demons.

"You can't have him."

As one, the Thunderbourne lunge an inch closer. I jump, drawing my grandfather's knife.

"You cannot have him." I repeat, threateningly.

All the shadows in the forest gather to the Thunderbourne, who sink into the power the shadows bring them, building up strength. They crawl along the ground. They mean to go under me, to get to Patches. I throw my grandfather's knife as he used to teach me on hot summer afternoons while my sister played with her dolls, whenever my parents discussed something serious.

It sticks in the ground, pinning a Thunderbourne down. The creature screams out in a voice that encompasses all the screams of the lives it took. My blood runs frigid to hear the thousands of lives, human and light and plant, all crying out at my hands. However, I do not move. I let the Thunderbourne squirm like a worm under the blade, twisting and distorting and screaming.

It doesn't die; I doubt it could, but the sight of it in pain makes the others back off. Their eyes do not betray them. I cannot tell if they are scared or merely rethinking their plan. I squat down in front of the Thunderbourne that is still writhing. It locks eyes with me and stops screaming.

"This one is to be left alone. You do not get this one." I growl at it. "Do you understand that?"

The creature stares at me with unchanging glow-in-the-dark-green eyes. They are not as frightening to me as they once were. I have nothing left to lose except this one last friend. I am determined to do right by him. I put a hand on the black handle of the knife and twist it once more sending the creature into a thousand different formless contortions, then withdraw the knife.

The creature returns to the comfort of the other Thunderbourne, and they all look at me. Good. Let them know that I am not to be used unwittingly anymore. Let them know that I can still protect life, that I am the one who will choose who they can claim and who they cannot. Let them know that I am their master, not their slave!

Patches groans. The Thunderbourne lock their stare onto him. I tighten the grip on my grandfather's knife. My knuckles turn white with the determination inside me to save this man. The demons do not attack. They fade away and I know that this is nowhere near over.

I turn to Patches. The blood drains from his face when he sees my knife.

"What are you doing?" He asks softly, the first words he's truly spoken to me since Cara's death. I suppose, to him, it looks like I am pondering the same course of action that she chose.

"Nothing. I… thought I heard something." I sheathe the knife.

"You can be honest with me, you know." He whispers, catching me completely off guard.

"What?"

"I know you've been lying from day one. But you don't have to. You can talk to me. You can tell me the truth."

"I haven't been lying." My confrontation has left me looking for a fight. "I told you what happened. I am from the Underground. I managed to surface and make my way through the Storm Lands from Skeleton to the Swampland to the Ruins and, now, to Strongwood."

"Yes. You did tell me that. It's not everything, is it?" His patient tone is infuriating.

"So?"

"You don't think I deserve to know the truth?"

"No." I snap. "Actually, I don't. You don't know me; you don't know what I've been through. It is my life, and if I do not want to share it, it is my prerogative to keep it secret."

"I may not know you well, but I do know you. I know you hate peas and that you talk in your sleep about a friend of yours whom you lost in the shadows of Underground. I know you've seen more death than me." He runs his hand through his hair. "And I know that you are keeping something important from me, maybe something that even concerns me."

"And you want to know what that is."

"Yes."

"How very chivalrous of you- how very white-knight of you. Oh, poor girl from the Underground, she must be terribly broken by her past. You think you can save me from that? You think that by hearing all the terrible things I've done that you can protect me from those memories?"

"I don't know. I want to try."

"I can't be saved. And the only reason you want to is because you couldn't save her, isn't it? Well, just so you know, I had a hero and he wasn't you- he will never be you- and he used to listen to me and sing to me when I wept- you don't even hear me when I cry- how many times have I wept along this road with you not two feet away and you never noticed. Not once. My hero is dead, do you hear? Dead. His body taken by the Thunderbourne and so I can't even give him my special coat or kiss his hand or even have the blessing of being washed in his blood. All I have is my memory of him, and sometimes that isn't enough to know whether or not I actually had him at all, or if he were just a figment of my fucking imagination. So forgive me if I don't readily hand out those memories to every person I meet!"

I'm inconsolable. He just looks at me with those eyes, those beautiful, brown, human eyes. I know I'm hurting him. I know I'm hurting myself. There is not a chapter in my life that can go by without me hurting someone that I love. He's the only other person in the world, and I am destroying him. I close my eyes and regain some shaking semblance of composure. I try to speak more calmly, more rationally, with strength and conviction rather than suffering.

"Look. You want the truth? In my world, there are demons. Death lingers in shadowy threats and haunting memories. I face the probability of poverty and the inevitability of utter isolation. And I'm fighting for life, for love, for the honest good of beings who need my help. And every time I try to help, they die.

"So if you want to stand in my way, you better stand tall. If you want to lecture me on the irresponsibility that is me, speak loudly. For I have no time for small bumps in this road; I will stomp them out without taking a second glance.

"But, if you do not want to ruin me, if you care for me, stand by me and let me make the choices I need to make to preserve you. Because that's what I'm doing, you can't save me, but, just maybe, I can save you. But you have to trust me- you have to trust that if I were to tell you what you think you want to know, you would kill me in a heartbeat."

He flinches. I try not to notice.

"Patches, you are worth everything to me as a friend. Please don't ask me to turn you into an enemy."

He stands up and opens his arms to me. This gesture summons the Thunderbourne, poised around him, ready to strike. I shake my head, although whether refusing his touch or warning the demons I cannot say. It occurs to me that, for as long as I stay with Patches, the Thunderbourne will hunt him. Either that or he will see who I really am. I can't ask him to watch the death of any more of his friends. And a voice inside me says *if they cannot have him, who can they have?* I know I will have to find someone to satisfy them, and soon.

"I have to leave you now." I tell Patches, casting my eyes to the ground. His arms fall sharply, slapping his sides. I flinch at his reaction. How can I be so strong and so weak at the same time?

"Why? Or do I not deserve to know this either?"

"No, you do." I can't deny it. He does deserve to know the danger he's in because of me. "The Thunderbourne are back. They've been following me through the woods. I'm going to draw them off."

His butterfly knives are out and flashing before I can finish my thought. Of course he is going to try to fight for me. Were it the other way around, wouldn't I insist that I could help him?

"My name is Celia. I want you to know that. I've never told my real name to anyone after the storms. That's the truth."

"We're crossing the stream together, remember? I can't let you face the demons alone."

"What is your name, Patches? Your real name?"

"No. I tell you that and you're gone."

I nod.

"Even if you don't tell me, I am going to leave. If I have to wait until you are asleep and sneak off, I am going to leave. If you bind me and drag me through Strongwood, I will convince the trees to help me escape, and I will leave. But I'd rather leave with your name in my memory so I can always remember that you are not a dream, that this journey was not just a figment of my imagination. Please."

"David. My given name is David. And you better not forget it."

"I won't."

I embrace David. I weave my fingers into his hair and tug on it a little. I bury myself in his heartbeat and breath. I fall into his warmth. I gather his light to me. I smell his skin until I know that I will never forget him. I indulge in the only goodbye I've ever been allowed.

Then I turn away. The hardest lesson I've ever learned, I've learned well. I do not look back. I live with the ache in my chest, I make peace with it, and I lead my army, my prison of Thunderbourne away from my friend.

Twenty-Three

I walk for what could be multiple wake-spans. I can always see the Thunderbourne around me. I can feel their hunger rising. I know I have to find them food soon or run the risk of them turning back to find David. This knowledge keeps my feet stepping through the leaves longer than I should be able to go on.

Eventually, they begin to attack the trees. I hear the soul of Strongwood cry out, and despite everything I've told myself about the necessity of the Thunderbourne's feeding, I cannot convince myself that my friends are only trees. I cannot abide the death of any life, be it creature or plant or light or idea. I summon every ounce of courage that I have left in me.

"Stop!" I command the Thunderbourne.

They oblige, turning to me mid-destruction. I feel their hunger as if it were a fog around the forest. I call it to me; I picture it gathering around me, clinging to me, dripping off every part of me. I am what the Thunderbourne want, not the trees. I am the life they lust after, the existence they long to feed upon and destroy. They are wolves and I, the prey.

I bolt. The chase is born. I run, reveling in the explosion of my lungs and the pounding of my heart. The adrenaline fills me. I run like I am running to see my family again, like Friend is waiting for me. It is my intent to run until I've drawn the Thunderbourne out of the forest, out of the ruins, and lure them into the waste so we all can die there. Of course, I do not make it that far. I fall while I am still in the forest. The trees draw away from me. I lay, laughing into the dirt. Waiting.

I know the exact moment the Thunderbourne catch up. I can see their eyes flashing even though all I can see is the dirt as I lie face down on the forest floor. But by now I know these creatures well enough to know that they've formed a circle around me, that they are turning into one hive-mind monster with an appetite for life. I will make a good meal for them. I will fight and I will struggle just like they want. In the end, I will become part of them.

I take a breath; they lunge.

It begins with tremendous pain. There is something that stabs through both of my shoulders ripping me off the forest floor so I stand before the greatest evil I have ever faced. It is more than I could have ever feared. A beam of edged light tears through me. The flash of lightning from the Thunderbourne's eyes finds every corner of my being. It sees me. I am completely vulnerable inside and out. I am naked before the demon in every way.

Something warm and sticky drips down my back from the shoulder wounds. I try to curl over myself, but the demon does not let me. It lifts me high into the air and drops me. My legs snap, but I try to run anyway. The dark, cold claws of the Thunderbourne catch me by my waist and lift me again into the air. This time it shakes me as hard as it can until I am a rag-doll, vomiting and crying and fighting back.

My spine becomes a dark treachery of burning. Terrible, expansive, fiery wings of black are born from my neck and shoulders, beating against me, consuming me from my spine inward. I writhe. I claw at everything: the wings, the hold at my waist, my own body. At first I am trying to free myself, but eventually succumb to just trying to hold on and steady myself until it is time for me to die.

I can't help but scream out for someone to help. I cry out for my parents, my grandfather, Friend, the old woman, Sights, Patches, David: every name in my memory is shrieked into the darkness until I am left begging trees and lights to help me. No one comes. I am alone. I try to take a breath through the knives in my lungs. I try to retreat into myself.

The Thunderbourne draws me close to its chest and bites into my neck. Every inch of me, even the dark wings I've grown, falls limp. My eyes cannot shut. A fly lands on one and walks across it and I cannot even blink to chase it off. I am screaming soundlessly, my jaw dislocated like the skeletons in the Ruins.

I am so sorry for everything. I am ready to die.

Just before my final, rattling breath, there is an abrupt release. The burning black wings melt away into a tingling in my shoulders; my legs are shaken but whole. The forest around me is as it has always been, vast and alive with the restlessly hidden fear of predators in the night. Death, the tease of relief, eludes me.

I swallow. I do what I have always done: I stand. A voice from far, far away, whispers to me: *"Don't look back. We are here, always, following you through the darkness. Trust what you know to be true. We can't reassure you with physical presence, but you have to keep going. Celia, don't look back for us."*

Then, like the green flash of lightning, driving humanity underground; like the last echo of the songs in the dark; like the faces of the fallen, one held breath bursts from my lungs and everything is quiet. I am alone, but not without. I am alone, but it is enough.

As I continue on, towards the heart of the forest or the edge of the world or whatever lies just beyond my next step, I think I can almost make out a glimmer of pink light through the rise of the branches before me.

Epilogue

We will not destroy her. We will wait and let her lead us to the rest of her kind. We will disappear and she will forget us. But we will not forget her. We will mark her, bind her to us with the black scar that now traces her spine from her neck to her hips, and we will watch her, unseen, in the shadows. We will not destroy her. We will make sure she survives. She will be the last of the living in this land.

Molly Katherine Miller has always been drawn to the art of storytelling, and has been writing since childhood. *So Echoes the Thunder* is her first book, inspired by her time living in New York City. She has written several plays, poems, and short stories, with no intention of stopping here.